Love Lia

Xox

A Novel

Written by Coral Cooper

Trigger warning

This book contains content that could be triggering to some readers. If you have been affected by any issues in this novel, please know that you are not alone. There is always someone who wants to help you.

You are loved.

This book is dedicated to everyone who has ever felt like they are not worthy of love. You are.

Chapter 1

Dear diary

Does love exist? Like is it possible to be 100% in love with someone? My role models for love haven't exactly been up to a standard that I would call love. I'm sure that my parents had a good run at things before I came along, but I don't remember my mum or dad saying it to each other or being affectionate towards one another.

I was 8 when they split up. Right before Christmas. Christmas was never the same again. It was always 'Ophelia are you staying at my house this year?' 'But you were at their house last year'. I see my dad every couple of weeks. Well recently it's been every few months. He got remarried and had three more kids, so he doesn't really have time to see me, I also don't have the guts to say that I don't want to see him anymore. I understand that he's my dad but anytime I'm around him I feel suffocated with emotion and afterwards I feel as though I have a big black cloud lingering over me. I feel like I turn into a different person, a sad, angry version of the usually bubbly person that I strive to be. My mum used to talk to me about it, but after nine years she knows that I can work through it on my own.

I adore my mum, she's probably the closest thing to love I can think of. She's worked her ass off since she was fourteen. She opened her salon when she was twenty, I was two. I think the fact she has her own business was very intimidating to my dad, which definitely egged on his arseholiness. I get my dad though. I wish that she were around more, especially when I was a kid. When I had a shitty day at school, when my bullies were especially horrible there would have been nothing more comforting than my mum by my side. My mum's name is Cherry Bloom. Which is ironic because I'm allergic to cherries.

Does love exist?

Love Lia

Xox

"What are you doing?" Dan says peering over my shoulder, slamming his panini on the canteen tables.

"None of your business Dan!" I snap by notebook shut.

Me and Dan have known each other since the first year in high school. We are on complete opposite ends of the popularity scale. I am on the more chill, arty, nerdy side where we basically sit like chips and wait for seagulls to eat us, while Dan, well Dan is a seagull, a nice seagull, but a seagull no doubt. His seagull friends gave me hell for the first two years of high school. They took my books out of my hands and threw them across the corridor. Dan ran to help me pick them up, as he kneeled down, he said 'wow, I never realised how pretty you are.' One McDonalds date and one very bracey kiss later we decided we were better off as friends. We always said hi to each other in the corridors, text each other and would hang out at mine if my mum was working late, but we never hung out at school until the beginning of this year. When all his ballbag seagull friends left school.

"New year party at mine on Saturday, are you coming?" Dans mum and dad must be on their monthly get aways.

"Why are you having a new year party, its halfway through January?" Dan isn't exactly the sharpest tool in the shed but that is a bit ridiculous.

"New years-themed party." He corrects me. What is a new year themed party you ask? I have no clue. But if Dan can find an excuse to have a party, he will have a party.

"Yeah, I'll ask my mum if I can finish work a few hours early." I work in my mum's salon after school a few days a week and on Saturdays. She puts me to work making drinks, sweeping, answering the phone. I love it though. I start my beauty therapy course in August so I can follow in her footsteps.

"Why do you need to work on a Saturday man?" Dan sighs. Dans mum and dad make really good money and have never put pressure on him to get a job, any plans for the future, nada. My mum makes good money too, but she doesn't let it get to my head, when I was thirteen, I was in the salon working. Even when I was little and would go after school, she'd have me cutting foils and wiping down the nail bars. I was never forced to go into beauty therapy just because my mum does it, I genuinely love it, it's so interesting. And on the plus side you get to make people feel beautiful and that is the best feeling ever.

"I'll be there in an hour Dan." I hang up my phone, applying my serums to my face.

Inspecting my face in the mirror, tweezing stray brow hairs, and shaving my peach fuzz. I got an early finish from work and spent it shaving my legs and washing my hair, you know one of those 'the showers' exfoliating, tweezing ingrown hairs from your vulva. I mean the booty cheeks have never felt smoother. I'm wearing a short dress so I'm talking no chances in a fluffy arse cheek peeking out. Just as I apply my cucumber sheet mask the shitty rain starts which turns the shitty attempt at snow into an even shittier slush. Central Scotland am I right?

Chapter 2

Dear diary

I'm looking forward to tonight. It's definitely not my scene or how I usually spend my Saturday nights but I'm excited. I've not glammed myself up for a hot minute. I'm very much a granny. I spend my Saturday nights on the couch, with an enjoyable book or watching a cheesy tv show that I've seen a hundred times over. 'friends' is my favourite. I've watched it since I was a baby. My mum said that when she watched it whilst she was pregnant, I would start kicking. They're just normal people, with jobs, going through the ups and downs of life, breakups, makeups. Can we just appreciate the fact that Phoebe is the best character. Her dad fucked off, her stepdad was in prison, she nor her family had any money, her mum killed herself, never had a good relationship with her sister. And even after all that she still ended up in love, with a roof over her head and I'm sure she ended up having a bunch of kids and her and mike turned into the von trap family. If she can do it anyone can.

Love Lia

Xox

I let my lotions and potions soak into my skin as I take my black, sparkly sequin dress off the hanger and take my black converse off the shelf, trainers are the new high heels after all.

Back in the bathroom the steam has now disappeared, I slap makeup on without thinking about it, I've had the same makeup routine for years, its what my mum taught me. I don't wear makeup to school, well not a full face of makeup anyways, a little something here and a flick of mascara there does the trick. I finish curling my hair just as my mum comes home from work, trotting down the staircase to show her my outfit.

"Oh, you look stunning my darling, come on I'll give you a run round, I don't want you wasting your hair in the rain." She says applauding me.

"Is it not a bit too much?" I push my boobs into place.

"Ophelia Opal, you are beautiful inside and out, and I can assure you that you're wearing more than everyone else your age."

My mum went through a lot of shit when she was growing up, constantly yo-yo dieting to make her mum happy. When she had me, she vowed to never comment on anyone's appearance in a negative way. The self-love and empowerment quotes all around the house really drill it into you. I'm a chunky gal, my mum likes to say 'an hourglass with extra sand' I do like my body. I've always had big boobs and a big bum which all the girls hated me for, and all the boys obsessed over. People in school. like to assume that I'm 'easy' 'a slut' 'a slag' just because I wear clothes that accentuate my body. I've just turned seventeen a few months ago and I've never had sex. In fact, my only ever kiss was with Dan when I was thirteen.

My mum has not been in a relationship since my dad when I was eight, she doesn't seem to care though, she doesn't show it on the surface anyway. I think the reason she's stayed single all these years was to protect me. Bringing men into my life when they might turn out to be just like my dad doesn't seem to be a good thing. My dad hasn't spoke to me in a while, I got a phone call the day after my birthday back in October. His excuse for being a day late was "It was Ryan's talent show, so we didn't get home till late." I've never even met his youngest son. He has three other kids- Ryan who's six, Oscar who's four and Lewis who's two. I try not to think about my mum and dads divorce too much. The more that I think bout it the more I feel like I'm nine again. My life is good now. And my mums life is good now.

I'd hate for another man to come into it and fuck it up.

Chapter 3

"You have a brilliant night darling! Phone me if you want a lift home!" My mum passes me a few cans of premixed cocktails in a blue polly bag. She's a cool mum like that.

"Thanks mum, love you." I kiss her on the cheek and jump out of the car.

I can hear the music bumping from the driveway, the neighbours definitely aren't going to be happy. Walking towards Dans front door I crack open my can of woo-woo and pull my dress down over my thighs. Dan sees me through the living room window and waves, by the time I reach the door he's standing in the hall waiting on me. At first glance I want to estimate that there's fifty people here. That might not sound like a lot but for me that induces an anxiety attack. Dan gives me a quick hug.

"How do you know all these people?" I shout in his ear as I close the door behind me. adjusting my handbag strap around me.

"I don't" He shrugs.

I make my way through the living room full of people, some from school, some are strangers and find myself a corner that seems safe and quiet.

"Oh my god, Ophelia!" I hear a loud squeaky, slightly drunken voice.

"Lacy, oh my gosh!" I throw my arms over her. I remember Lacy from primary school, we used to read together all the time at lunch before she moved to a different school, her curly hair gets in my smile as I hug her.

"Oh my god, are you okay?" She laughs, unsticking her hair from my lip gloss. "How have you been? Tell me everything." She tucks her hair behind her ears.

"I'm doing okay." That was a lie. No one is okay anymore. I struggle to make friends and pretend I don't want any to protect myself from them leaving me like they inevitably would, I am trying to find who I am in a world that tells me who I should be, I have a different version of myself depending on who I'm around and I sometimes get confused as to which ones really me. But that doesn't seem to have the same ring to it. "What's been up with you I haven't seen you since we were like eleven." It turns out that Lacy had to switch schools because the head teacher was being *cough cough* racist towards Lacy and her family. Tell me you live in an uncultured neighbourhood without telling me you live in an uncultured neighbourhood. Lacy ended up getting an early conditional offer at university for this year to become a physicist!! My pending beauty therapy degree seems pretty under whelming next to that. However, beauty therapy is so much more than just painting nails or giving facials. To know about hundreds of ingredients and chemicals, being able to tell from someone's nails if they have an under active thyroid. Pretty sure only beauty therapists know how salicylic acid works on the skin and how it helps prevent and reduce acne. It goes into the pores and swirls around like a tornado and pulls out any gunk. Very disgusting to think about but amazing to learn about.

I keep folding my fingers on top of one another just like I used to do when I was a kid. Glancing around the room, overwhelmed at everyone's presence. "I know something that'll cheer you up" Lacy smiles. I look up. "That's Brian, he goes to my school, and he hasn't stopped staring at you since you walked in… and if you don't go over and introduce yourself, I'll go over and do it for you."

I look over at him, very clearly an athlete, my guess is rugby, his stance takes over the couch. Brian bites his lip, looks me up and down and ushers me over with his finger. This is strange, I'm not used to receiving such obvious attention; especially from people who look like him. Lacy pushes me over to him, I take a gulp of my second can of cocktail, this one is strawberry daiquiri.

"Hi." I smile. He's traditionally handsome, tall, dark hair, dark eyes. Which I'm not sure if I like or not. The world says I'm supposed to like it.

"Hey, I'm Brian." He takes my hand from my side and shakes it confidently, as if he's a CEO of a company and his hand is used to holding wads of fifty-pound notes.

"Ophelia" I shake his hand back.

"Oh, like the song" His voice croaks.

"No" I say defensively. That is the one thing about my name which I don't like. People assume I'm named after the song by The Lumineers, I like to think the song is named after me.

We start chatting, you know the usual small talk pish which usually makes me cringe. I was right he is a rugby player; he seems really nice, he keeps complimenting me, which is something I'm not used to, I'm so used to being pushed to the side. He's very masculine which again I'm not sure if I find attractive.

"It's a bit loud down her, do you want to go up the stairs?" He leans into me when he says it.

I nod.

He takes my hand and leads me out of the living room. I look back at Lacy to give her the eyes (ladies, you know what I mean) only to see her snogging the face off Dan. They do look like a good match to be fair. There are a few people drinking on the stairs that I almost fall over. My dress creeps its way up my thighs with every step. Brian is still holding my hand, which I think is nice. I stop walking when we reach the top of the stairs, but Brian leads me into Dans bedroom. There's two spare rooms and he takes me to Dans. Brilliant. I adjust my dress again as I walk into the room. Yup definitely regret wearing this. Brian shuts the door behind him. I look over at Dans comic book bookshelf and the multiple action figures that are sprinkled around the room, how that man was ever popular I'll never know.

"So, tell me more about rugby." I tap my toes to the beat of the music. Trying to make this situation casual, acting like it's a very normal thing for me for boys to take me into bedroom when in actuality it has never happened before.

Brian turns around to me, slowly approaches me as his hard eyes look me up and down, putting his hand to my face once he's close enough. My face moves closer to his and our lips meet. I put one hand on his shoulder as we continue kissing, his tongue slides across mine. One hand on my face the other on my waist. The kissing gets more intense as he starts making his way down my neck, which can't possible taste good because of the amount of perfume I'm wearing. We begin to lower ourselves onto Dans bed. He's a good kisser, I can't lie, well better than Dan anyway, *Lacy must be having the time of her life downstairs.* Brian is confident in the way he kisses, a little too confident if I had to give his critiques. He starts to slide his hand up my thigh and under my dress. I tremble feeling his hand grip my thigh harder.

"Brian, don't do that." I pull away. "Brian, no, stop." He ignores me. He starts to pull my dress up further, kissing my neck as he does it. "Brian, stop." I try to move away from him, but I can't. This is it. I'm trapped. "STOP!" I shout, I try to push him off me but before I know it he has me face down on the bed, Dans covers muffling my cries for help. My wrists pinned above my head; he uses the other hand to slide my thong down to my knees. I can feel his hard-on on my thigh. I try to scream but nothing comes out. Brian forces his dick inside of me roughly and fast. I can feel the air get thinner and the tears get thicker. He keeps going. 'It'll be over soon' I keep repeating to myself. 'It'll be over soon' he keeps going. My wrists can feel his hands tightening, my back can feel all his weight crushing me. Brian groans, still inside me. He pulls himself out of me and pushes me onto the side. I have no thoughts. I hear him buckle up his jeans and he leaves. Shutting the door behind him.

…

I lie, frozen, crying, exposed, in pain. I don't know how long for. I look up at Dans wonder woman figure with guilt, feeling like I've let her down. I sit up, shaking with fear, pulling my thong and my dress into place, my crossbody handbag still on, the strap strangling me. I want to leave this room, but I also can't. My eyes are streaming, I can still hear the music pounding. I bring my wrists in front on me, the red marks start to come out. What just happened?

Chapter 4

I remember when I was younger, my mum would always tell me that 'no one has the right to your body' and I believed her. I don't believe her anymore. A part of me that was mine was taken. And it felt like Brian had the right to take it. He done it so confidently and abrasively. Like it was obvious that I was there for him. Like I was a free sample in a supermarket, and you take two instead of one because they're there for you to take. That's how I felt, that's how I feel right now. Like a toothpick with a slice of peperoni and cheese on it.

My phone is in my handbag that still feels like is strangling me. Why could I not have done anything to stop him?

Me- Dan, help your room.

I can still feel his hands, his hands, everywhere, I can still feel…him. My heart pounds, my mind goes numb, my body feeling nothing but everything at the same time. I can still taste his whiskey in my mouth and his body on my back. I always thought that that would never happen to me, I'm way to cautious, too strong, I can fight people off, but in that moment, I couldn't do it. Did I deserve it? Why did I go up the stairs with him?

Knock knock

I'm back again.

Dans door creaks open, Dan peers around the door and scans the room, his eyes unravelling the events. I look over at him, tears soaked through and snots dripping down my face. My dress still wonky. "What happened?" He asks softly, closing the door behind him. My tears start streaming again. I don't know what happened. I don't have enough words in my vocabulary to describe the monstrosity or pain and darkness that occurred moments ago.

"I don't know" It's true, how can a consensual, passionate kiss turn into- that. Well, he didn't actually ask to kiss me. I didn't ask to kiss him either. "Brian… he" The words taste bitter as I scrape them from my tongue. "He raped me" I whisper through my cries thinking that if I say them quite enough it's as if I haven't said them and if I didn't say them then it didn't happen.

"Can I hug you?" Dan asks, crouching down beside me. His voice comforting and his presence calm.

I nod, still crying. Dan wraps his arms around me slowly. I rest my head on his shoulder.

"You're safe now. Do you want to phone your mum?" I don't think Dan knows what to do. I don't know either. I shake my head. I just need to think. I let go of Dan, I can't imagine what my mum would do if she saw me like this. *Going on a murder spree comes to mind.* I need to process this before I can leave. I trust Dan, he's seen me at my worst, this might be my new worst. Dan has seen me ugly crying over the stress of exams and the stress of my dad, but I don't think that anything can compare to this. Helping your friend process the fact that she was raped.

"Give me ten minutes. You can stay here tonight if you want." Dan stands back up and leaves the room. His knees cracking as he does so. I pull Dans duvet covers over myself wishing that they would just swallow me up, so I don't have to be here.

I look at myself in Dans full length mirror opposite me, I was once, so innocent, so trusting, so delusional. Why did Brian do that to me? What possessed me to think that he would want to have a normal conversation? Why did I go up the stairs with him? Why did I not see if coming? The inner feminist knows that I done nothing wrong, but I can't help but imagine if I done something different, pushed him off of me sooner, screamed louder before my face was imprinted in the covers. I can hear commotion downstairs, the front door opening and closing, bottles clanking together.

Some length of time passes, I couldn't tell you how long. Dan comes back into his room, and everything is now silent. He brings me a pair of pink pyjamas. "You can take a shower if you want, everyone's gone."

"I'm so sorry Dan, I didn't want to ruin your night." I feel really bad.

"Lia, you haven't done anything wrong, I'll make up the spare room for you, take your time he places the neatly folded pink pyjamas on the bed and leaves the room, closing the door behind him.

I slowly ease my way out of the room, one step at a time, the house is silent apart from Dan ruffling bedsheets across the hall. The bathroom is bright and white which is migraine inducing, a fresh white towel is on the heated rail. The rainfall shower head makes to room fill up with steam. I begin to undress myself, slowly peeling off the wonky dress whilst looking in the mirror. I hate myself, every fold of skin, every blemish, every beauty mark, it doesn't feel like mine anymore like I'm watching myself from another point of view, it feels like his. My face goes under the water first, like lava it numbs me. I can feel every pore open as the water hits them. I sit down. I don't know why. Standing up feels like too much effort. Cupping the water between my hands. I take one of the shower gels from the side and take the gently used loofah and start scrubbing. Usually, I'm not a big sharer of sponges, loofahs etc but needs must. I can still feel him. I bubble up a bar of soap in my hands and start washing my vagina. It hurts. By this point if fully lying down, my eyes have no more tears. I snail like, piece by piece stand up. Foetal position, sitting, kneeling then finally stand. The cool tiles send chills through my legs as my feet grip onto them. I squeeze my hair over the shower to get the excess water out of it. The caramel spaghetti looks like it's been dragged through a bush. The towel is warm and feels like a hug. It's very obvious that no matter how pristine this bathroom is, its clearly Dans. As I rummage through the cupboards to find a spare toothbrush I come across a very dusty, unopened box of condoms that he probably bought on his sixteenth birthday. My hair still wet I put on the pyjamas; they smell like baby powder.

I shuffle my way out of the bathroom, to find Dan, sitting cross legged in the hall. "Hi." I look down at him.

"Sorry, I didn't know if you'd need me. Come on, I've got the room ready for you." He groans as he stands up.

I take a glance downstairs and it looks like he's cleaned up, or he's just shoved it all into a cupboard to worry about later. It's sweet that Dan waited outside the bathroom for me. Dan is the one person that I can count on. He has always been there. He has grovelled over the fact that he remained friends with arseholes that bullied me. And he regrets that he didn't stand up for me. But that's all in the past, he's here now. That's what's important.

The spare rooms blinds have been shut, the covers drawn back, my handbag on the bedside table, the warm lamp is on, a glass of water, a cup of tea and two slices of toast. "I told your mum you were staying over." He looks over at me. I look up at him. "Don't worry I just said that you were staying over."

"Thank you" I don't want my mum to know what happened. I lean over to Dan, my head on his body and his hand by my side, he hugs me back, rubbing his hand over my wet tangled hair. I feel safe with Dan. We've been proper friends for four years. He has never once made me feel uncomfortable, said anything that hurt me, apart from being friends with shitty people back in the day he's a good person. Those boys that bullied me have no idea how much they impacted me, they broke me. I would purposefully take the long way to class, go to my mum's salon during lunch so I wouldn't run into them, I stopped speaking in classes that they were in with me. Constantly, every day, they'd ask me out, jokingly, they'd put their arms around me, make pet names. It doesn't sound like bullying, but it really hurt me. Brian reminds me of them. Brian would have joined in with the bullying. "Right, I'm going to go finish cleaning up." Dan lets me go, kissing my head.

I climb onto the puffy pink bedsheets. I feel too sick to have the toast, so I opt for a few sips of the tea before it goes completely stone cold. I take in the room. This is

Dans mum Stacey's mini retreat for when her husband is annoying her. Her reading nook is it the corner, floor to ceiling shelf full of books. Stacey is a big business lawyer which must be really stressful, I never see her without a book in her hand, or in her handbag. Reading is an escape. One day I'd love to have a room dedicated to books, a library style room with the ladders on wheels, my Ikea billy bookshelf will do for now. Stacey's dressing table is under the window, her luxury fragrances discoloured from the sun.

Knock knock

Dan cracks the door open. "I'm going to bed now, are you okay?" He says softly, he's wearing his superman pyjamas.

"Can you stay with me?" I whisper, I don't want to be alone. Not right now.

"Yeah, do you want me to lie next to you?" I think he's going to ask me everything from now on. Clicking the door closed.

"Please." I whisper softly, my voice croaky and stuffy from crying.

He goes under the covers beside me. "Do you want to talk about it?"

I turn over to my side so I'm facing him. "Not particularly… why do people do things to hurt people?" Every man, my dad, those bullies, Brian. Besides Dan but trust me he has had his moments, my mum sometimes, but she tries her best to make up for it. Everyone who has came into my life has hurt me in some way, shape or form. People are supposed to come into your life to make it better, like a handbag, handbags pull together an outfit, adds that pop, and holds some of your shit.

"Lia." I look up at Dan. "You are such an amazing person, you have your life ahead of you, you are working so incredibly hard to achieve your goals, you are so kind to everyone, you are a ray of sunshine, you see the beauty in everyone. You don't need anyone to come into your life to make it better, you can do that yourself." Dan is my handbag.

"Thank you." I whisper. "Can you hug me please? I ask as a tear drops onto the pillow.

"Of course." Dan slides one arm under my head and the other under my arm against my back to hold the back of my head. He kisses my forehead whilst I gently rest my head on his chest. Feeling his chest rise and fall.

We lie like this all night, occasionally waking up to my eyelashes brushing against his top or to him snoring. I usually remember my dreams. I don't remember last nights.

Clank

I wake up to the sound of Dan clanking the plate of soggy toast and the cold mug of tea together. "Sorry." Dan whispers trying to tip toe. I look at the alarm clock. 9:24am. There's a part of me that wishes that last night was some sort of lucid dream, but it wasn't. I lie in bed for another few minutes. "Here's some of my mums' clothes" Dan sits a bundle of clothes on the vanity. "Don't worry about bringing them back, my mum loves you more than me."

"No, she doesn't." I sit up brushing my hair out of my face, rubbing my eyes as they adjust to the light.

"She does." Dan sits at my feet. "Literally anytime I bring you up in conversation she goes on and on about how amazing you are." I don't know if he's kidding or not, but I adore his mum, she's so cool, so on top of her shit, plus she makes banging dinners, her mac and cheese is to die for. "How are you feeling this morning?" He puts his hand on the covers that cover my shin.

"I'm okay." There's that lie again. But if I say that I'm okay maybe subconsciously I will be, the universe will manifest that I am okay. If I lie over and over again maybe it will come true and I will in fact be okay.

I get myself dressed in Stacey's overpriced fluffy grey lounge suit, the soft, velvety fabric feels like a kitten and head down the stairs. Dan makes me more toast. I sit on the comfy armchair and stare at where Brian was sitting last night. I hear the click of the kettle. Dan brings through a beautifully presented breakfast, all perfectly placed on a pink and white polka dotted tray. Two slices of toast soaked in butter cut into big triangles and stacked against each other, a mug of milky tea with three sugars and a stack of rich tea tea biscuits. With a spoon on the side of course in case the biscuits flop into the mug. I smile at him when he sits the tray on my knees. "Thank you." Breakfast like my gran makes. My gran is the only member of my dad's family I still speak to. I don't think she likes my dad much anymore. My gran is another safe place. If were out for a meal and I finish my plate before her she insists on giving me some of her food even though I'm full, she carries around a freezer bag of mint imperials in her handbag everywhere she goes in case anyone wants one. I have picked up some of her little quirks like that.

My bag for school is full of hand cream, perfume, deodorant, baby wipes in case anyone needs anything, and if I get bored my bag gets flung onto the table for some self-care time for me and everyone around me. Surprisingly her and my mum still get on well. It makes me think I have a happy family for a few minutes.

Fuck.

"He didn't use a condom." I blurt out dropping a biscuit into my tea. What the actual fuck. He didn't even have the decency to wrap up his cock before shoving it inside of me. Okay, it's only been twelve hours I still have sixty until I'm too late to take the morning after pill. I'm in no mindset to go to the chemist right now. This is something I need my mum for. It sounds stupid to need your mum to go with you to get the morning after pill but I don't want to go alone and I don't want anyone else to go with me.

Dan peers at me over his cup of coffee, unsure on how to answer me, when to answer me or even if to answer me. I don't want an answer.

"Thank you so much for taking care of me Dan." I wash the few dishes in the sink. I can feel my manic state coming. This happens when something shitty happens, I feel sad some a few hours then I go insane. "I'm going to head home." I dry my hands on the dish towel before picking at my eyebrows.

"I'll walk you." Dan takes a sip of his coffee before putting it on the worktop. "Come here." He holds out his arms. I fall into them. "Go home, have a shower, have a sleep, then do what you need to do." He claps my hair, holding me to him.

It's only a ten-minute walk to my house. The smell of greasy fry ups floating out of the opened windows fill the street, a trail of beer cans trails out of Dans driveway.

"How did you get everyone to leave last night?" I pick up a few cans and toss them into the outside bin in the driveway.

"I told them my mum and dad missed their flight and were coming back home." He laughs and puts his hands in his pockets to hide them from the cold. "Where is your dress?" He asks adjusting his glasses.

"Oh, I put it in the bin." I start walking faster. I don't want to look at that dress again. I don't want to be reminded of what happened when I was wearing the dress. I adjust my handbag tighter around me.

"Why? You looked amazing in it." He follows closely behind me. "It's not your fault you know." Dan looks at me as I turn around. "You're not to blame, you done nothing wrong, the dress wouldn't have changed what he did." I know it's not my fault, the uber feminist inside of me knows that the dress didn't mean I said yes and that everything that happened last night has nothing to do with me and everything to do with him. Dan takes a deep breath. "If anything, it's my fault. I shouldn't have invited people I didn't trust." He looks at the ground.

"It's not your fault either Dan." I latch my arm through his as we slowly walk along the pavement.

We reach my house and hug one last time before I go inside. "If you need anything let me know." He says waving me goodbye. I stand at the end of my driveway for a few minutes. I just need a few minutes until I can face reality. Because right now I'm pretending that it didn't happen. I just need for it to not have happened for a few more minutes. Just a few more minutes.

Chapter 5

Today is Sunday, which means that my mum is manically cleaning. That's been her routine for as long as I can remember. She always starts in the kitchen, then works on the downstairs and works her way up to her bedroom all whilst doing loads of washings and singing and dancing to R&B.

The sound of the door closing behind me echoes the hall. The smell of disinfectant is in my lungs and the early two thousand hip hop is in my ears.

"Hi honey bunch." My mum shouts from the top of the stairs waving to me. "Did you have a good night?" She wrings out her mop, wiping her forearm across her forehead which is dripping in sweat.

"It was okay" I start making my way up the stairs. Dragging my feet on every step, clinging to the banister to pull myself up, like every step is a mountain. "I feel like shit, I'm going to go for a shower then have some alone time." I don't know if I should tell her. Is telling your mum you were sexually assaulted a thing? It shouldn't be a thing. It should never be a thing,

My room is cosy and fluffy and everything I want and need right now. I flop down onto my beanbag next to my bookshelf. I sit for a few minutes. My diary is on the table next to me.

Dear diary

I was raped last night. I don't know what else to write. I don't know if it was my fault or not. I don't know why I went into that room with him, or why I kissed him back, or why I didn't scream louder. I don't know why he did it. Why are men arseholes? I don't think I want to fall in love. It would be so much easier if I was attracted to women. Brian, that's his name, I don't know his last name, he plays rugby, he has dark hair and dark eyes and he's around six foot three inches, I know he's seventeen, but he might be eighteen I don't know his birthday. That's all I know about him. Why did he feel the need to rape me? Did I do something to suggest it? Were my words 'stop' not clear enough for him?

I don't know how to feel about it. He didn't use a condom, so I need to get the morning after pill then possibly get an STD test. We'll see if I start scratching.

I want to have the whole teenage romance thing, but I don't see that happening. Fuck love.

Love Lia

Xox

I can still feel him. It's the same feeling as when you feel someone staring at you, that lingering sensation. It's as if Brian is watching me shower. I'm fully lying down, letting the water batter my stomach, I put the bottle of shampoo over the drain so I can have a mini bath. I know I don't feel good when I do this, puddle showers I like to call them. Raspberry and coconut scents fill the room whilst the three-inch-deep bath keeps me company.

Knock knock

The knocking startles me. "Ophelia, it's just me." Mum cracks the door open. "I've just finished cleaning, Chinese and movie night?" She asks hopefully and happily, the complete opposite of me.

The shower head fills my mouth with water, I spit it out. "Yeah" I open my eyes. "Mum, could you take me to the chemist?" I sit up, the hours are ticking in my head.

"Of course… can I ask why?" Her voice goes higher. Completely clueless.

I turn off the shower, wrap the towel around me and open the shower door. I want to tell her, but it's scary. *Deep breath.* "I need the morning after pill." I start to tear up. Staring at myself in the mirror opposite me. I can see my mum's reflection in the mirror. It wouldn't be a big deal needing the morning after pill in any other circumstances because accidents do happen and my mum would be the first person I'd tell, but this is so… painful. "I… um, I was…" That feeling of last night comes over me again and erupts through me, up my throat until I'm screaming crying in a fit of snots and salty tears. My mums arms huddle around me, her hand in my dripping wet hair. You should never have to tell your mum out of all people that you were raped.

"It's okay, your safe my darling." She kisses my head.

I can't decipher the tears from screams. "I was raped mum." The words are bitter and hurt to say. Mum leads me out of the bathroom, arms still around me, she's crying, she cries when I cry. Every emotion that I have ever felt explode and come out all at once.

"Listen Lia." She takes my head in her hands and stares at me. "You're safe now. Do you need me to do anything?"

"He didn't use a condom." I bubble. The thought of him inside me makes me sick and the possibility of his sperm crawling around me is revolting.

"Okay. What WE are going to do, is get you dressed, in some comfy clothes, get your hair dried, get you feeling better, go to the chemist. Do you want to go to the police?" Still holding my head up in her hands. My mum is good at this. She's good in these kinds of situations, so smart, she knows exactly what needs to be done and how to make me feel better.

"No." I've seen the statistics. Less than one percent of reported rapes lead to jail time. I already showered, threw away my clothes and I'd assume that Dan has washed his sheets after finding out what happened in them. So, there wouldn't be any evidence. It's weird how I've thought about that. I shouldn't have to think about that.

"Okay. That is your decision. I support you. Then were going to get a Chinese takeaway and watch whatever you want on the telly." Her tears are dripping now too.

"Thank you, mum." I sniffle into her shoulder.

I gulp down the half full plastic cup of water, the pill grazing my throat. There's nothing I want more than to leave this excuse of a private room (an aquarium glass box with a tea towel for a curtain) and go right back into my mums' arms, where I feel safe. I think the whole act of taking the morning after pill is humiliating. And it shouldn't be.

Leaving the display case to go to the safety of mum.

Chapter 6

My mum was never around for a lot of my childhood, it's the one thing I would change about her. I'm pretty sure I could count on my hands how many times she's cooked me dinner after school. After her and dads divorce, she worked twice as hard, she was out of the house at eight thirty and back at nine. She would drop me off at school and tuck me into bed. There were a few times where I'd do my homework at the salon when my gran couldn't watch me after school. She took a step back from the salon once their divorce was final and my dad stopped stirring the pot. She would pick me up from my grans at six then we'd go home. But she wasn't really home. She would do all the admin, reply to messages. I think the house felt empty once dad left. They were together since they were thirteen, the typical high school sweethearts. They didn't know themselves separately because they were always together. Maybe that's why I don't have a high school romance, I've seen it at the other side. My mum and dad were different people when the met versus when they split up. Fourteen years they were together, and I think it was around year ten they slowly started to resent each other. I'm sure my mum hates that she stayed in an unhappy marriage for so long. And she knows how much it hurt me. Her parents were in an unhappy marriage for nine years. It hurt her, more than she wants to admit. All she wanted was to have a proper Christmas. One where she didn't have to go between houses to make people happy, everyone but herself. And she tried her best for me to have the family she wanted growing up. But sometimes things don't work out.

"Okay, Chinese is here." Mums sweet voice sings, spinning around two white polly bags. She told me I was couch bound for a few days. "I've taken the week off of work." She says dumping the bags on the coffee table.

"What?" The only time off my mums taken in the past year was when we went to the log cabin in the summer.

"We can have the whole week together. No work phone, no school." She dishes out the fried rice and rips open the bag of prawn crackers.

I smile. "Thank you." I'm looking forward to spending the week with her, just chilling. Its very rare that we spend quality time together. The time we're together most is at work. Which isn't ideal when she's, my boss. A good boss. But my boss, nonetheless. I want to spend actual time with her. Not be passing ships in the night that barely know each other. A proper mother and daughter who have spa nights, movie nights more than once a month, bake together when it's not Christmas. Bond on more than a mother and daughter level.

"I was raped." She looks over at me. "I was fifteen."

"Mum, I'm so sorry." My fork bangs on the plate. "I had no idea." I can see the torture in her face when the words stumble out of her mouth.

"It's okay, I came through the other side of it. But it took me a while." She plops herself down on the couch at my feet. She can feel me wanting to ask questions. "Drunk guy, at the school toilets at the valentine's day dance." Her breath is harsh. "We all have a story. Everyone has story.

It still doesn't make it okay." Her sincerity is calming. She went to the police, to court, he got out of jail after a year for good behaviour and went straight back in after raping and murdering his little sister. Sick bastard.

"How did you begin to feel better?" I can't believe my mum went through that and I had no idea. That's why she knew what to do today.

"Your dad." She packs a prawn cracker full of chicken choi mien. "And... a lot of shopping. It took weeks before I could sleep without him there." My mum loved my dad. She needed him. It's good to know that they loved each other for a while. My dad was her person. Until he wasn't. My mum and dad loved each other. I was the creation of love and adoration.

Dan- Hi, you okay? X

Me- Hi. Yeah, I'm going to be a hermit for a while btw, mothers orders. X

Dan- I'm here if you need me, on a good note me and Lacy are chatting now. X

Me- Good for you, don't fuck it up. X

Dear diary

Everyone, at some point, has a person. A person they fall for, a person the think about all the time. My mum had my dad. Dan has Lacy (fingers crossed, I'll need to get the inside scoop.) I've added lacy on social media, I've not had a proper girl friend in a while and I think about her a lot, I missed her so much when she moved schools. But anyways most people have a person. Someone they can be themselves around, be comfortable around, have not nervous kisses, find themselves together. I observe people at school, there's flirting, the PDA. There's someone for everyone. Will I find my someone?

Love Lia

Xox

Well, my mum was right, shopping fills a hole in your heart, I haven't looked in the mirror since I walked out of the shower on Sunday. It's Thursday. And I haven't left the house for more than ten seconds to collect a parcel from the front step. My mum has left the house though, to get the food shopping and to probably make sure the salon hasn't burnt down without her. We've spent the last few days going from my bedroom to the bathroom, to the living room, then back to my bedroom. Mums been sleeping in my bed with me, otherwise I feel watched.

I take the blanket off my bathroom mirror and inspect my naked body. I'm looking at myself through my eyes for the first time in five days. It's not so bad, but I better get myself in order before I go back to school on Monday. My mum says I don't need to go back yet, but I'm weirdly missing it. I miss the normality of it all. The good thing about going back to school is that no one there knows what happened.

Its Sunday now. Which only means one thing. Full body
'the shower' I don't lie down this time. I sit.

Dan stays beside me most of the day, like a human shield
protecting me from people. I can get out of my own head
when I'm here and get into other peoples. The teachers.
Those who can't do teach. There's a very small handful of
teachers that enjoy their jobs. One of which is my English
teacher, the creative writing part is great but I'm awful at
the evaluative essays. The curtains were blue because the
writer is conveying depression. No, the curtains are blue
because they wanted them to be fucking blue. Miss
Fitzsimons doesn't care that the only part of her class I
enjoy is creative writing. I have a knack with words, my
gran tells me that a lot. Then there's the majority of
teachers that bang on a power point and call it a day.

Dear diary

*I've been back at school for a few weeks now. I like it.
That's something I'd never thought I'd write. It's not the
socialising, it's the actual schoolwork itself. I'm handing
in all my homework, I'm working at the salon more, my
exams are coming up soon. The one I'm dreading the most
is maths. There are parts of it I understand and parts of it
that I don't. I've been trying as much as I can, but maths
just isn't for me. There's a part of me that doesn't want to*

be a beauty therapist like my mum, I still want to be in the beauty industry, but I'd love to work with companies, social media management, I don't know we'll see.

I can look at myself again. I'm slowly getting my personality back. I'm curling my hair again, adding some pizzaz to the school uniform. But I'm still quiet, I'm always quiet though. I'm an observer, I'm also a nosy bitch but that's beside the point. I need to go and do some homework for my business class. That's one of my favourite classes. I think. Let's hope I figure out my life.

Love Lia

Xox

My mum dropped me off at school this morning, which is unusual now. But I like it. I have a free period first thing this morning, I'm not too nervous about my exams but I want to do well, it won't define my future, but I want to be proud of myself for something I never thought I'd achieve.

The energy of the school seems off. Like I'm there at the wrong time, well I am here a few minutes earlier than normal. So maybe this is what school is like at 8.27am. I glance around once I take a seat at the windows. The 'popular girls' strutting across the school with their matching skinny lattes, matching hair, matching handbags, clones of each other. I genuinely couldn't tell you who's who. It's strange, disturbing, being churned out like little robots.

"Morning Lia." Dan waves as he walks through the doors. "Guess what."

"Morning Dan." I smile. "What is it?" I puff. Sipping my travel mug of coffee.

"Me and Lacy are going out this weekend." Grinning from ear to ear. Having a little boogie. "We'll need to find you someone so we can double date." I think that once he said it her regretted it because he didn't wait for my reaction. "How was work on Saturday?" He never asks me about work. We begin walking to class. My eyes explore the corridors.

The bell rings as we get there. That's when I see him. An angel, sapphire blue eyes, dark hair, his soul golden yet edgy.

I feel my heart light up.

Chapter 7

His eyes are like an ocean, they meet my eyes like honey.
His radiant smile glows. His name is now angel man.

Angel man is standing next to the classroom door, I grin
back at him. Angel, me and Dan are the first ones in line
to get to class.

"Hi, I don't recognise you." I don't know why I said that.
I think there's a spoon full of confidence instead of sugar
in this cup.

"Hi, yeah, first day, I'm Blake." Blakes voice is rough yet
sweet.

"Ophelia, that's Dan." I point to Dan who's paying him no
attention whatsoever. Dan is reading the posters on the
walls as if they're new when they've been up for four
years, and we have walked past them thousands of times.

"Oh, so the song was written for you?" His laughs are
songs.

"Very funny, most people call me Lia." My voice tightens,
defensive at his words.

"Your name is beautiful Ophelia." It sounds ever nicer
coming from him. My throat relaxes after he appreciates
my name for my name and more than a lyric from a song.

Miss Ramage comes running down the corridor, coffee in
hand, apologising for being late, it's still only me, Blake
and Dan waiting to go into the classroom. Miss Ramage is

my registration teacher, she makes sure we're all here, gives out letter etc. She's one of my favourite teachers, probably because she's not much older than us. She always looks so nice, she gets her brows, nails and lashes done at my mums' salon and she always has bright red lipstick on. We make our way into the class once she unlocks the door. Dan finally notices Blake.

"Who's the new kid?" He whispers to me; Blake makes his way over to Miss Ramage's desk.

"The most beautiful man alive." He probably heard that.

"Double dates then?" Dan elbows me and chuckles.

I smile at Dan. We take our seats as students begin to trickle in. Blake comes over to us and sits across from us at our table. No one ever sits next to us, the chalk and cheese of the school. Me- dorky, loner chick and Dan- ex-popular dude, secret comic book nerd. It does make a lot of sense that we're friends now that I think of it. Dan is just dorky in private whereas I could ramble on for hours about how amazing Phoebe Buffay is or how underrated certain books are. I don't think that Blake matches our vibe. He seems edgy, yet soft, sour yet sweet. For a few moments I forget about what happened a month ago. It's been on an ongoing loop since it happened. Some days it's all I can think about and others it's muted and on in the background like a tv show that you've seen ten times over. But not friends, friends get our full attention one hundred percent of the time, and I will laugh and cry every time I watch it and I expect everyone to be the same, no exceptions.

"So, Blake. What brings you to Clyde high school?" Dan draws my mind to him.

"Oh…um, me and my mum just moved. I'm here from St Marys." As he says it my stomach drops. That's Brian's school. I wonder if they know each other, I wonder if Brian bragged about it to him.

"Oh. I'm surprised we haven't met; I threw a party last month and a bunch of St Marys students were there." Dan can feel me begin to zone out.

I'm back in his room, I can feel his breath of the back of my neck, his hands around my wrists, his dick inside me. I start to bite and shake my lip, staring into the abyss. I can feel everything, every thrust, everything. Dan knocks my knee with his under the table. I snap back. I wipe a tear away from my cheek. The immediate feeling when I snap back is strange. Like when you're having an intense dream and you wake up and you're not sure if you're still dreaming or not, and instead of knowing your awake because the dragon is gone, I know I'm not dreaming, because if I was dreaming, what Brian did to me wouldn't have happened.

Dear diary

There's a new guy at school, his name is Blake. He is beautiful, he's in my registration class, business class and art class. We chatted all day. I like him. I like him and that scares me. I've never liked anyone like this before. Yes, I've had crushes, people I've found attractive, but Blake has a light inside of him that I'm drawn to. I want to spend more time with him. He's really interesting, he's moved around a bit, he's going to college in August too, he's going to study barbering. He works evenings at the fabric factory. He has dark brown hair and icy blue eyes, he's about three inches or so taller than me, he was wearing a black leather jacket, he has a few ear piercings that strangely match mine. Oh, and he went to school with Brian, so I shouldn't like him. I should stay far away from him, I didn't ask him if he knew Brian, if I did, I would have had to explain it. I'm definitely not ready for that, I'm not ready to be involved with anyone romantically either. I want to be ready, but I'm not. I see the couples at school, and I get jealous. I want to be in love, but I don't see that happening. I'm not sure I'm capable of falling in love or for anyone to fall in love with me. Holy fuck, Blake just added me on Instagram.

Love Lia

Xox

---

blake.robinson101 started following you

I follow him back; I drag my teeth along the inside of my lip.

Blake- Hi Ophelia, thanks for being nice to me today. X

What does that mean?

Me- Hi Blake, thanks for being nice to me today too. X

Blake- Can I ask you something? X

Me- Go for it. X

Blake- Are you are Dan together? X

Oh my god as if!!!

Me- Oh my hell! No, we did go out for about a week 4 years ago, but no, platonic with a capital P. x

Blake- okay. X

Blake-…

He stops typing. Why did he stop typing? Is he gay? Does he like Dan?

"Hi Huni, I'm home!" Mum shouts, slamming the door behind her.

I come running down the stairs, my mum has done some food shopping, I help her get the bags to the kitchen. Unpacking the freezer stuff, planning out my meals for the week.

"Mum?" I fold the reusable bag.

"Yes darling." She opens the wrapper from the bananas and puts them in the fruit bowl.

"How did you become okay with liking dad after you were assaulted?" I shouldn't have phrased it like that.

My mum is in a trance after I said that. "Well, um." She takes a deep breath. "I had to learn my own boundaries, and then I had to teach your dad. We weren't intimate for six months." She takes another deep breath. "Why is something going on?"

"There's a new guy, I think I like him." I bite my lip while I smile. I don't want to be smiling, it's scary.

"Do you want my advice?" She asks, pulling out a bar stool.

I nod.

"Get to know him. But you need to love yourself before you can love someone else. If things progress and you and him become an item, know your boundaries, that's true to any relationship." My mum knows her shit. "But go for it, you've got nothing to lose." If I ever need advice or opinions on something, I go to my mum, she is the best at it. "And you're a fucking prize."

How do you make a move? Blake is sitting next to me; we're sharing a water cup to wash our paint brushes. He's good at painting. This is my final piece that's getting sent away to be graded. It's a watercolour still life of a book, candle and some amethyst and rose quartz crystals. I've called it, self-care. I can feel Blake shake his leg under the table.

"You, okay?" I ask him, whispering.

He turns his head to me, smiling showing off his dimples. "Yeah." Nodding.

"Good." I say tilting my head up to him.

"Are you okay?" He puts his head on the table so he's looking up at me. This man is adorable.

"I like sitting next to you." I turn my attention back to my watercolour. I think that's a move.

"I like sitting next to you too." He moves his leg closer to mine under the table. I think that was a move.

It's been a week since I met angel/Blake. I've thought about him every day, I've sat next to him for about twenty hours. That's twenty hours or leg touching, chats about life. Our art class is where we chat most because it's just us two at the table and the table is at the back of the room.

My phone pings. "Shit, my dad just texted me." My dad hasn't text me since new year when he wished me a happy new year. Blake looks at me confused. "We don't see each other much." I sigh before I unlock my phone, being careful to not let the teacher see.

Dad- Hi, haven't heard from you in a while, how's it going?

Me- Hi, I'm okay.

How is it my responsibility to have a relationship with my dad? It would have been so much easier if he just fucked off and I would've just slowly forgot about him, but instead he reaches out every few months and I remember him. Just enough connection to tell himself that he's not a shitty dad. I'll never forget all the arguments, all the fucked-up excuses to why he didn't pick me up when it was his time with me. I was always the last on his list.

1-him

2-his new wife

3-kid 1

4- kid 2

5-kid 3

6-golf

7-me

Deep down I care, but I don't show it, I'm good at not showing it, for a while anyway, then I break. I just cry myself to sleep when it comes flooding back to me. The fact that no matter how much I want to be. I'll never be my dad's top priority. I've had to come to terms with that over the past few years. I slowly started to wait outside for him for less and less time, until I didn't even bother to put my shoes on, because I knew he wouldn't show up. My mum doesn't know the number of times he didn't show up. I would always make sure she was at work if he was supposed to pick me up, because I didn't want to be around her when my dad let me down, because it would let her down. And it would hurt her. She thought she had a daughter with a good man, a man that would show up. But she didn't. She trusted him. I trusted him. I don't trust anyone anymore.

Although I think I want to trust Blake.

Every time I look at Blake, I want to kiss him. Which is scary. The last kiss I had led to something I didn't want. But I think I trust him. I haven't told him my boundaries; he hasn't given me a reason to give him my boundaries. I think he knows I have them though, that's maybe why he hasn't kissed me yet.

The shower is steaming up the bathroom. I just got finished with work, so I'm covered in a mix of nail dust and acetone. I trace my hands over my naked body and close my eyes, over my neck, my shoulders. I want Blake to be here. I stop at my wrists; I can still imagine them being pinned down. My waist, my ribs, I want Blake to touch me. But not where Brian touched me.

I used to sleep naked a lot, I would go to bed in clothes then just slowly pull them off before I went to sleep. I go to bed naked tonight, climbing under the covers, hugging myself at the waist as I fall asleep.

Chapter 8

Dan has not stopped talking about Lacy. It's cute but it's making me jealous. I've made it as clear as can be that I don't hate Blake, so why has he not asked me out? I would ask him out but that's out of my comfort zone a teeny bit.

"Dan. Would you want a girl to ask you out?" I'm half listening to Dan and half staring at Blake ordering his lunch at the canteen. Lip reading 'panini' before he hands over a handful of change.

"If you mean, do you think you should ask Blake out? Then definitely." He takes a bite of his panini. "He likes you, but he's scared of you." He takes another bite, scrunching the wrapper, saying the fact that Blake is scared of me so casually.

What the fuck. Scared? "What do you mean?" I ask defensively.

"You don't give a fuck about other people opinions of you, you're not one of those pick me girls. He's used to girls changing for him and being at his beck and call. He still likes you, but he doesn't know what to do."

"How exactly do you know this?" Still annoyed.

"He told me." He smiles, shoving the last bite of his panini in his mouth.

Blakes now right next to me. This is weird, I can't imagine anyone being scared of me. I'm a sunny, sunflower, sunshine person. I don't do anything intimidating. Although my mum did say that guys used to be intimidated by her, her unneedyness and independence used to scare silly boys away. Maybe I'm not the sunshiny person that I think I am. I used to be a sunshiny person; I haven't felt like a sunshiny person for a while.

There are a few things I've noticed about Blake. He's gentle, even with the small things like clicking his pen lid on, he does it so gracefully, like he's frightened he's going to break it. He's a gentle gentleman. He holds doors open for me when we're going into classes and smiles back at me when I smile at him. He has a soft centre, like a marshmallow, behind his hard exterior he is a teddy bear.

Blake- Hi, are you busy? X

My homework gets thrown to the side. My stack of notebooks cascading down to my bedroom floor.

Me- Hi, no I'm not. X

I am.

Blake- Do you want to go for a drive and grab dinner? X

Blake's the only guy in fifth year who can drive and has a car, which automatically makes him attractive.

Before I know it, I'm tying my laces and jouging up my hair. I don't know if this is a date. Is it a date? He didn't say it was a date. But for two seventeen-year-olds, driving around in a car is the hottest a date can get.

Me- Ready in 5. X

Blake- I'll pick you up. X

Anytime I see this scene in a movie I cringe. My mums working till eight tonight, so I have four hours until she's home.

Blake parks his blue Corsa at the bottom of the driveway, I was watching for him from the living room. He's getting out of the car as I jump out the door, locking it behind me. Blake comes round to the other side and opens the passenger side door. It's the little things like that that make me believe there are good men. "Nice ride stud." I laugh. His car is clean. There's something about a man and his first car. You can tell a lot about a man by how he treats his car. If his car is dirty and unkept he doesn't care about the little things like holding doors open. He makes sure to hear my seatbelt click before he starts the car.

"Where to madam?" He puts on a posh voice, and I laugh as he revs the engine.

"KFC me lord." I put on a posh voice too.

We take the rural back roads through the farms and fields. I want to tell him how I feel and that I like him but that I'm not ready to like anyone. "Uh, Blake." I say quietly.

"Ophelia?" He says sarcastically.

"Is this a date?" I look up from my knees at him. "Cause if it is then that's okay." My voice and words soft in case the reply is hard and painful, because then it might not hurt so much.

He deepens his breathing. "Do you want it to be a date?" He looks over at me, taking his attention away from the road for a few seconds.

I nod.

"Then yes. This is a date." He turns his attention back to the road. I smile. This is a date. This is my ideal date. Not because it's with Blake but a long drive and a takeaway is my ideal date. And yes, because Blake's here.

Chapter 9

The drive to KFC is mostly silent, I pass Blake my debit card and he refuses to take it. The smell of gravy and grease is incredible. Blake takes us to a quaint park with a car park attached to it. We pull the seats down and clumber into the back seats. I feel the butterflies in my stomach flutter when I'm near him. I really want him to kiss me. But I also don't think there's anything I'd hate more,

"I really like you, Ophelia." He says as I pull the bucket of chicken out of the bag. Our eyes connect, the deeper I investigate them the deeper I fall. Blakes eyes are sad by my lack of response.

"I really like you too Blake." I whisper, we both smile. My breath quivers.

"Ophelia, can I kiss you?" No one ever asks that. I like that Blake asks that.

"Yes." I take a deep breath and lick my lips; Blake tucks my hair behind my ear with one hand and clasps my cheek with the other. His touch is kind, endearing, lovely. He leans in slowly, teasing me. Our lips brush against each other softly. My heart glows. He pulls away, I open my eyes. I feel tension build up in my chest, I want to kiss him again. I lean into him and move my lips around his, placing a hand around his neck. He kisses me back gently. Our lips are connected, we become one, our energies mix to become a ball of electricity. He brings one hand to my waist. That's scary. I pull away.

"I'm sorry." He says realising I've stopped the kiss.

"I'm sorry." I shake my head. I can still imagine Brian, touching me. "I. Umm…" Brian kissing me.

"Are you okay?" He reaches for my hand. I can feel tears build up, taking me back to that night. My wrists raw and sore, the sound of him grunting, the feeling of being slowly suffocated by the covers.

I'm back.

Why the fuck did I do that? I really wanted to keep kissing him, I didn't mind that he touched my waist. I wanted him to touch my waist. "Um, something, happened. to me, a few months ago… and I'm still not okay…" I let go of his surprisingly soft hand and cross my arms and lean my head against the back of the passenger seat. I'm embarrassed. "I'm sorry, I should go." I begin to open the door; I swing my legs out. Blakes hand reaches for me.

"Stay." I turn around to face his sad eyes. "Ophelia, I want you to stay." I swing my legs back round facing him and close the door. The rain starts tapping on the windows. "Talk to me." He puts his hand next to mine, I place my shaky hand in his. Our rings touch.

"I was…assaulted." A tear falls to my cheek. "And this is scary for me." I pull my sleeve over my hand and wipe my tears away. I feel vulnerable speaking about this.

"Ophelia. I'm so sorry to hear about that." His hand tightens around mine. "Do you want to eat our dinner before it goes cold?" He grabs the bucket of chicken from the centre console and puts in between us, still holding my hand. "I really like you, Ophelia." I really like that he says my name so much, and how he admits his feelings so casually and that it doesn't tear him apart inside, because that how I feel when I admit my feelings.

"Why Blake?" He looks at me confused. I've never understood how other people can like me. "Why do you like me, Blake?"

He takes a bite of chicken. "You are beautiful, your brownish greenish eyes are like heaven." He takes another bite of his chicken. "The way that when you smile you look down, you smile a lot, especially when you think that no one's looking. You are passionate about everything you do." Okay he's listing things. Boak. "The way your life is so simple, yet so mysterious and you don't let anyone in." The rain is battering off the windows. "The way that you are so god damn beautiful, and you don't even realise." His voice gets quieter as he lists. I trace my finger nails up his arm and rest my hand on his shoulder, my eyes follow the beauty marks on his face and every hair in his eyebrow.

"Blake, can I kiss you?" I say half leaning in already. "Yes Ophelia, you can kiss me." He whispers. He brings both of his hands up to my face, steering clear of my waist. We both inhale shakily and stare at each other for a moment. He's terrified to kiss me first. I close my eyes and press my lips against his. Barely pulling away to exhale, his tongue sweeps along mine. Blakes hand is in my hair.

"Is this, okay?" He asks, briefly parting our lips.

"Yes." I'm sure of it.

I'm not sure how long we kiss for, but our chicken is stone cold, and my lips are chapped and I'm out of breath.

"Thanks, you for being nice to me Blake." I buckle my seatbelt.

"My pleasure madam." I chuckle when he puts on his posh voice again. I like him and I don't think I'm scared. I'm not scared that Blake will hurt me, I'm not scared that Blake will rape me. He didn't move his hands away from my face/ neck. Physically I was throbbing for him to touch me. Touch me everywhere. But that's still scary. "I have a secret." He says as he put his hand on the passenger seat to back out of the empty car park. "You can't laugh though."

"What is it?" I'm intrigued.

"I'm traumatised from blowjobs."

My jaw drops. I didn't expect him to say that. "Further information is required please." I wave my hands.

"So, it was about six months ago, first girl I had ever started seeing." He tightens the grip of the steering wheel. "Things were going well. We had hung out a few times, blah blah blah. She invited me back to hers. Things start getting a bit frisky, we're basically naked, but I told her I wasn't ready to have sex. I go down on her as a gentleman would." That's a picture I'm excited to see. "And so that happens, she says she wants to go down on me, never given or received oral sex until this night by the way." He points his fingers, making it a point that this was his first time. "So, she, you know, and, you know. It's great, I look down and she." He balls up his first and starts to boak. I'm laughing at this point. "She, bah, bah." He composes himself. "She has crisps stuck in her teeth. Bah." Blake takes a second to hold back the spew.

I am in bits, hysterically cackling. "What happened? What did you do?" Crying with laughter, slapping the centre console to stop myself from pissing my trousers.

"Fuck knows. But next thing I know I was home scouring my dick and scrubbing my mouth out. She never spoke to me again after that." He starts laughing with me now. "And I couldn't eat crisps for weeks."

That is by far the best thing anyone has ever said. It's the first time Blake has opened up about his past. He doesn't talk about the past very often.

Blake takes my hand between gear changes. "So, Ophelia." He laughs as he breathes. "Would you, maybe, want to start going out with me?"

That's scary. Going out with someone means that there are expectations and eventually a broken heart. I don't know why but I say "Yes." Something inside my heart forced that word out of me. No matter what's happened to me, how fucked up my views of relationships are, I like Blake. And I like that he likes me. I don't want to question it. I am going to allow myself to like Blake and enjoy liking Blake.

Chapter 10

We pull into my street. "Fuck, that's my mum's car pulling into the driveway." I ball my fist up and cover my mouth. My mum would never be angry about me going out with someone. But she would be annoyed that I didn't tell her, not because she wants to know where I am all the time but because she wants to make sure I'm safe. She was one of those parents that wouldn't let me stay at a friend's house unless she knew their parents. It's safe to say I didn't have many sleepovers growing up.

Blake stops at my driveway, my mum notices it's me in the car as she's locking her car door, she waves. "Do you want to come in?" I ask, it would be weird for him not to say hi to my mum after seeing her. And after she sees him dropping me off from all she knew was a dogging session.

"Sure." He unbuckles his seatbelt before me. He runs around to the other side of the car and open the passenger side door. I could get used to this princess treatment. I am Blakes princess in this story. His damsel in distress, a woman who wants to learn how to heal. Blake wants to heal me. Why? I don't know. I don't want to question it; I just want to enjoy it. I like how it feels when I'm around him, I realise this whilst we're walking up to my door. I like that I like Blake and I like that he likes me.

"Hi mum." I can hear my mum dumping her handbag in the kitchen. "Come on through Blake." Blake nervously wipes his feet on the door mat. You never realise how cluttered your house is until someone you like walks in and you remember that pile of washing that needs put away or the glass that you left on the work top.

"Hello darling." Mum pretends she doesn't notice Blake walking behind me.

"Mum this is Blake." I put my hands in front of Blake, presenting him like a piece of art. Which he kind of is.

"Good evening, Miss Bloom, it's really nice to meet you." Blake reaches out his hand to shake hers.

"Oh, please Blake, its Cherry." She smiles, walking towards him, holding her hands out for a hug. "It's so nice to meet you." I nervously grin watching it happen. I hate romance movies and love romance books for this reason, everything is so much more natural and amazing when you imagine it in your head and in person its awkward as fuck. Mum smiles at me whilst she hugs Blake. "Do you want to stay for a quick drink Blake?" She asks, parting their weirdly long hug. Blake looks at me now too.

"That would be lovely, but I need to get to bed, I'm working till late tomorrow, thank you though." Blake smiles, I like Blakes smile. "It was so nice meeting you Cherry." I smirk walking past my mum to walk Blake back to his car. I can hear my mum clapping like a child back in the kitchen.

We reach the front door, Blake looks me in my eyes, then down at my lips. I like his lips. I look at his eyes, then his lips. I melt into his body. This is the first time I've hugged Blake. He's good at giving hugs. His arms wrap around my arms and onto my back, rubbing his hand above my bra strap. I look up at him. He looks down at me, I close my eyes and we kiss again. I like kissing Blake, because it's not just kissing, its trust. I trust Blake. "I'll see you at school tomorrow, Blake."

"I'll see you tomorrow, Ophelia." He smiles. Giving me one last hug before he leaves. The door closes, I lock it. I can hear his car leaving the driveway.

I miss him.

I miss his face.

I miss his lips.

I miss Blake.

I miss who I am when I'm around Blake.

The house feels empty. My mum smiles when I make my way back into the kitchen. My mum likes him. Almost as much as I like him.

Dear diary,

I like someone. I've kissed someone. I like that I've kissed someone. That someone has a name. His name is Blake. Blake Robinson. I can't wait until I get to see him tomorrow. I know that I'm going into this too fast, but I don't care. I'm going to enjoy it. I never thought I'd meet someone who I could enjoy liking. I'm still scared though. Scared of liking someone so much I don't know who I am without them, liking someone so much I grow to hate them. Just like my mum and dad did. When we kissed in the back seat of his car, I wanted nothing more than to kiss him. Brian stopped me. Just for a few minutes. But Brian still ruined that for me. I don't want Brian to ruin anymore kisses. Especially kisses from Blake.

Love Lia

I lie in bed, happy. I haven't felt happiness in a while. But I feel lonely at the same time.

I smile going into school this morning, I still haven't told Dan about last night. I don't think I want too though. I don't want to put pressure on anything. We've kissed three times, it's not as if we're getting married. Three amazing, gentle, chocolatey kisses. Three kisses that didn't make me scared.

"Good morning, Ophelia." I recognise his voice, his amazing rough, sweet voice.

"Good morning, Blake." I reply, spinning around to face him. His beautiful face. "Can we keep this chill? For now?"

"Of course, darling." His words make me blush. "But I really want to kiss you again." He leans into my ear and whispers. I take a deep inhale, biting my lip. I want to say *I want to kiss you too Blake.* But Dan joins us. Oblivious to social ques as always.

"Hello peeps." Dan says cracking his knuckles. He can sense something is going on because he moves his eyes between me and Blake. He raises his eyebrows. I nod. He nods back. I smile.

Its Friday today and I have tomorrow off, for the first time ever. Literally. Me and Blake haven't kissed since Wednesday when we went on a drive, when we had our first kiss.

Blake- Hi, do you want to go out tomorrow, on a date? X

Me- Hi, yes x

Blake- Okay, I'll pick you up at 12 x

Okay, this is a date. What do you wear to a date? I don't want to ask him. But as I'm rummaging around in my wardrobe I settle for my blue frilly dress, with my blue cloud cardigan and my white boots. Still casual but also dressy. I'll be really embarrassed if he turns up in a pair of joggers.

I haven't gotten dressed up since Dans party. I missed getting dressed up. I haven't been anywhere to get dressed up though. The most I've done on a daily basis is brush up my brows and curl my hair when I've washed it. I wear tights under my dress to cover my patchy fake tan and to also not lead him to any expectations, I don't think he expects anything from me. In fact, I know he doesn't, or he would've asked me. I send a selfie to my mum to show off.

Mum- You look glowing baby. I love you so much. I get off work at 4 today, I'll see you soon. Xxx

Me- Thank you mum, I have no idea what we're doing so I'll text you when I'll be back. Love you. Xx

I wait for Blake at the living room window again.

Waiting.

Waiting.

Waiting.

He's late.

I'm annoyed. I hate tardiness. Its 12:09pm when he phones me.

"I am so sorry Ophelia." I can hear the tears in his words. "I'm coming, I'll be five minutes. He's panicking. "Blake, what's wrong?" He hangs up. I'm scared now. Pacing. Pacing. Pacing, in the living room. His car pulls into the driveway, I can see him crying when he gets out.

Knock knock

I run to unlock the door. "What's wrong Blake?" I open my arms to him. He cries into my shoulders. Wrapping his arms around me tightly. The front door still open. I shimmy him over and close the door.

"My dad." He cries. Sobbing. What is wrong with his dad? He has never mentioned his dad to me before. We make our way over to the couch; Blake is still clutching onto me. "He found us." He looks up at me. His eyes bloodshot. I have never been more confused in all my life. But now is not the time to ask questions and be nosy, now is the time to comfort Blake. I hold him in my arms, his head is on my thighs, tears all over my dress. I run my hands through his hair until he calms down. What has broken him? What is scaring him? Being broken and scared is my job, not his. I want to fix him.

Chapter 11

"He found us." I have no idea what he means by that. Blake is still crying, his head on my thigh and my dress creeps its way up.

"What do you mean?" I have no idea what he means. I rake my fingers through his hair, his dark, soft, fresh hair. I console him. It makes me uncomfortable that his head is on my thighs, but I don't think that's important right now. He cries into my legs, the bottom of my dress covered in salty tears. His hands on my thighs.

"I'm sorry." He says sitting up, wiping his nose with his fist "I shouldn't have touched you."

"Blake. What happened?" I ask. I don't care about the fact he touched me I just want to know what happened. I want to make sure that he's okay. He sighs like he doesn't want to tell me. Like it's something he's embarrassed of. I have so much shit going on I am in no place to judge anyone. "Blake. You can tell me anything." I hold his head against my shoulder. He gulps harshly and strains his breath.

"I haven't seen my dad in four months." He lets out a deep breath. "The last time I saw him, I walked in on him," He pauses and quivers his breathe. "Raping my mum." He throws his hands up to his face, shielding me from seeing his tears. "He battered the fuck out of me for trying to stop him… we left that night and didn't tell anyone. And when I saw him crossing the street, I had to take a minute to not get out and kill him… I phoned my mum to make sure she was okay"

"Oh Blake." What the fuck do I say in this situation. I mean my dad has done some shitty things like cancel plans with me last minute, not pick me up, be a general shitty person but he would never lay a finger on my mum or me. "Blake. I am so sorry that you and your mum had to go through that." I kiss the top of his head. "You should never have had to go through that." He starts full on crying. Blake has such a strong and hard exterior, but he's broken too. He grips onto me, I console him, starting to tear up myself thinking about it. "You're safe now." I speak. Those word hit me like bullets. It wasn't long ago someone was saying those to me. Blake tells me that his mum told him that it had been going on for years and she didn't want to leave because of him. I will never understand why parents stay in relationships for their kids' sakes, it's never going to end happily. The fact that Blake is damaged makes me think that we're more alike that I originally thought.

Blakes head is on my chest for God knows how long, my hands run themselves along his face, tickling his jawline with my fingernails.

"I'm really sorry for ruining tonight. You look beautiful Ophelia." He moves his face to face mine, sniffing the remaining snots from his upper lip.

"You didn't ruin anything Blake." I was *really* looking forward to going out with him tonight, but I'm just glad that he's here and he's safe. It means a lot to me, that after seeing someone who tortured his mother for years and assaulted him that his first reaction was to come to me. That means a lot to me. His sad eyes stare up at me.

"Can I kiss you, Ophelia?" He whispers, moving his body off of me, giving me space.

"Yes." I whisper back. Our lips already touching. Our lips move around each other's mouths, appreciating every sensation. Smiling between kisses, Blake's lips move around to my cheek and down my jaw. I lean myself back so I'm lying down, bringing Blake with me. It feels so good to be so close to someone. My hand rake through Blake's hair, his hands on my face feeling everything. My hands move to his arms, his arms move to my hips, his lips move to mine.

Wait.

No. I don't like this. I'm back there. I'm in Dans bedroom, Brian is suffocating me. I start gasping to breathe. I can't breathe. Panting. "Ophelia." Blake gets off of me. I'm trembling, I can't move. "I'm so sorry, are you okay?" I'm crying but I can't feel myself crying. I'm not here anymore. I can feel Brian watching me. Blake pulls me up, I collapse into him. "You're safe now." There are those word again. Those damned words.

I'm back.

"I'm sorry Blake." I'm crumbling. Blakes arms wrap around my back, all my weight is on him. "it's just."

"Don't be sorry. What's wrong?" He cuts me off, holding my shaking body close to his.

I rub my hands over my face. "Well, I already told you that I was assaulted." I look into his eyes. He's sad again. "I can't stop thinking about it anytime anything happens…"

"Do you want to talk about it?" He tucks my hair behind my ear.

I don't. but I continue. "His name is Brian. It was at Dans party… we went up the stairs and started kissing. He took it too far… I told him to stop." *Breathe Ophelia breathe.* "He didn't stop. He pinned me down. And raped me." No matter how many times I go over it in my head there's no way to describe what happened with words. There should be a new dictionary for shitty things that have happened to you. "I had never had sex. Or had a proper kiss before that night." I feel heavy when the words fall from my tongue, saying those words drain me. Every time I say those words or think those words, I feel like I'm going to pass out from exhaustion.

Blake takes my face and points it towards him. "Ophelia. That wasn't sex. That was rape." He holds me closer to him. "I'm sorry that that happened to you." Planting a kiss on top of my head. "You don't need to worry about me hurting you, Ophelia. I would never do that to you. And you didn't deserve to be hurt." Everything that Blake is saying is everything I've ever wanted to hear since it happened. No matter how many times I tell myself that I didn't deserve it, it sounds so much more real hearing it from someone else. Especially Blake. "I've never had sex before either. So, I'm not in any rush. To do anything. If I get to spend ten minutes in your company, I am happy." This man really needs to stop being so perfect.

"Thank you." I sigh, sniffing the snots back up my nose.

"Thank you as well." We cuddle on the couch, no television, no music, no speaking, just the odd cough or deep breath as we hold each other.

I guess we're both a little fucked up.

As much as Blake says that he doesn't care about sex and doesn't mind waiting, I want to be ready. I want to be able to have sex. I want to be okay with Blake touching me.

Chapter 12

The best part about taking exams is that you get to have study leave. Basically, you don't need to go into school unless you have an exam. It's a three week period where you only need to go into school one to three hours a day maybe twice a week, it's the greatest invention. The idea behind it is that you study. I haven't been doing much studying, I've either been working or hanging out with Blake when he hasn't been working. Blake is coming over today, after one of his exams. I told him that I wanted to make him dinner, which is a very housewife, nineteen-fifties of me, but there's something so romantic about making a meal from scratch for your partner, putting so much attention into making a meal, and it probably won't turn out how you expected it to, but they'll eat every last crumb because you put so much effort into it and they appreciate it so much. And they'll come to the door with a bunch of flowers and a box of chocolates. Because that's what Blake has done.

"Hello beautiful." He grins at me, pink roses and a box of milk tray in hand. He looks so glamorous compared to me. He's dressed up in a smart shirt and nice jeans, fresh shave and it looks like he's just had his hair cut this morning. A very big contrast to me. I've got my hair in a bun, joggers on and covered in flour and my top has a smear of gel polish down it.

"Hi handsome." I look him up and down in awe. He's so pretty. I usher him in and press my body to his. He is warm. Still with my arms wrapped around him our lips find each other's. "I've made honey chilli chicken with rice, and I've got cookies for dessert." I smile up at him.

"Okay that sounds incredible." He seems really impressed. I won't tell him that its literally honey mixed with sweet chili sauce. That can be my secret. He hands the flowers and chocolates to me. "These are for you."

"Thank you." I say it quietly, facing the floor. No one has ever bought me flowers. I never had a valentine's day card, secret admirer leaving me notes, nothing. I don't know how to react. I can't help but blush when I walk the flowers to the kitchen to get a vase to put them in, admiring the fact that the blush of the petals is similar to my cheeks. "I'll just put the cookies in the oven the now." Still grinning from the flowers. I set the timer. "Do you want to see my room?" That sounded really strange. Like it's a corny teen movie *do you want to see my room?* Followed by us running up the stairs on our hands and knees.

"Sure."

I quickly try and do a mental scan of my room; I don't think there's anything there that shouldn't be. He walks behind me as I try to nonchalantly go up the stairs, trying extra hard not to fall. I've never had a man in my bedroom before, in fact I hate people going into my room, it's my space and that's what I like about it. My mum hardly goes into it and that's saying something. I go into my room first, there's no washing piles, no dirty cups. But my diary is sitting out. Shit. I go over with my back to the desk and close over the notebook, crossing my legs as I turn around. I don't know why I keep a diary, it's just a way for me to get out my most personal intimate thoughts that I can't say to anyone else. It's nerdy very pre-teen of me but fuck it. I glance at Blake as he enters shortly after me, he was probably looking at the quotes and pictures on the staircase that my mum has plastered all over the house. He trails his fingers along the spines of my books on my bookshelf.

"Well. I never thought I'd be in Ophelia Blooms bedroom." He laughs turning around to face me.

"Blake. Can you do something for me?" I bite my lip, uncrossing my legs.

"Anything." He replies, moving closer to me so there's only a few inches between us.

"Can you touch me?" He scrunches up his eyebrows. "I want to be okay with you touching me."

"Okay." He takes a deep breath and looks me up and down. He gives me his hand; I hold it close. I let it go. I push out a breath. I play with the edge of my t-shirt and pull it up and over my head, my pink bra against me. I look down at my body and up at Blake. His eyes trace across me. "You're beautiful Ophelia." Blake takes his shirt off too, I watch as he carefully unbuttons his shirt. Gawking at his physique.

"I don't want to have sex." I blurt out.

His shirt drops to the floor. "That's okay. I just didn't want you to feel exposed." This is usually another moment in the movie where I pause because it becomes too cringey. My hands go to my stomach. I go over to the edge of my bed and sit, Blake follows. Throwing myself back so I'm lying down, Blake does the same, his head narrowly missing the wall. I lie with my eyes closed. I take Blake's hand and put it on my chest. His touch is what I want, my jaw tenses and my eyes flicker when he spreads out his fingers so his whole palm is on me. "You're safe Ophelia." Blake whispers, I can feel him adjusting his weight on the bed. "What do you want me to do?" Asking as if I have answers, because I one hundred percent feel like an idiot right now and that Blake will definitely run out of this room right now. "I'm not going to do anything to hurt you." His lips touch my forehead.

I relax.

"I don't know what I want." Blakes fingers play with the bow on the front of my bra. "I want to be okay." I don't know if I'll ever be okay again. I don't think I've ever been okay. Even before what happened with Brian. I've always had a screw loose and Brian just fully undone the screw and threw away the screwdriver. My stomach ripples as Blake's nails tickle me, going between my chest and my belly button. His soft touches bring me comfort. But all I can think about is how damaged I am. "I'm really sorry Blake. You shouldn't need to do this."

"Ophelia. If I need to lie here half naked with you to make you feel comfortable, I will do that every day. I admire you so much. And the fact that you want me to be the one to lie here with you means more to me than anything else ever could. I want to fall in love with you someday so if I need to be here with you and hold your hand whilst you work through all the shit going on I'll be here forever if you want me to be." He says it in one breath, pausing because he doesn't realise what he said until he said it. "I'm sorry. I shouldn't have said that." He rolls onto his back, staring blankly at the ceiling, hoping that I don't say anything else.

"Blake. I want to fall in love with you too." I admit. That is scary.

Chapter 13

Three months later

Dear diary,

I'm so happy that I finally have a close girl friend. Me and Lacy are going out to Glasgow today. She needs to get a few things for starting university, I still can't comprehend that she's going to be an actual physicist, with letters after her name and everything. She's moving to Stirling university, so I won't see her as much as I do now, I see her around once a week or at least try to video call her. It feels good having a proper friend again. I haven't had an actual close friend since Lacy and I were friends in primary school. I always had trouble finding friends, everyone was interested in superficial things like new body sprays or one of the ten years old boys' new haircut. I can never say that I'm not a girly girl, because I am, like its literally part of my job to be girly. But I'm more subdued and relaxed about my girliness. I think growing up in a salon when there were always women being women, I realised quickly that being super into body sprays or a specific lip gloss just wasn't me. In high school, I bounced around friendship groups and settled on being myself most of the time. I would spend a lot of lunch times in the library either reading or studying. I had a good relationship with the teaching assistants because they would spend their lunch times in the library as well, one of them in particular, always went out of their way to talk to me and I went out of my way to talk to her. She would always help me in my maths class, and we would say hello to each other in the corridor. I'm going to miss not seeing her.

Oh my god. I haven't even caught you up on all that's happened in the past three months. Sorry I've been busy. So, Me and Blake are planning on falling in love, no matter how ridiculous that sounds, it was really sweet. But it really terrifies me. I read a poem by Shakespeare once...

You say you love the rain, but open an umbrella

You say you love the sun, but you find a shady spot

You say you love the wind, but you close your windows when it blows

That's what I'm afraid of when you say you love me

No matter how much you love someone there will always be a part of you that hates them. Even if it's something stupid, like you hate the way that they fold towels when they put them away. Slowly but surely that hatred will build until you don't want them to fold towels anymore. Sure, they might be some people that can one-hundred percent love someone and that is also terrifying, how can you be so enveloped in love that you can't find something that irritates you? Anyway, me and Blake really like each other. Me and Blake are getting really close. Every make out session gets easier for me to handle. There has been some... under the clothes action. Which was hard for me. Blake told me that we can take it as slow as I want, but he doesn't understand. I don't want to take it slow anymore.

I got a promotion at work, kind of. I've taken charge of all of the online marketing and social media. So, I schedule posts, help my mum set up her training academy that she's opening up soon. I've taken my personal social media a lot more seriously now as well. I love making people feel good. And that's what I want to do forever. Wither that be in a salon, or giving people self-care tips online, I should definitely follow my own advice to be fair.

I passed my exams!!! I got my results in a few days ago. I got a C in English. (Thanks to my creative writing essays for getting me that fifty percent) a B in business. Those were my two big exams that I put pressure on myself for. I got a passing grade for all the others, which is good enough for me. I start college next week; I don't know if I'm excited about it though. I want to do beauty therapy, but ever since working on the behind-the-scenes stuff for my mum I don't see myself working on the front of the business anymore. I find the science behind things interesting of course but I want to be running stuff and actually being a boss bitch. That's something I need to figure out.

Let's hope I finally get a track of my life.

Love Lia

xox

By the time that Lacy arrives at the train station we need to run to make the train, we don't even have time to have a hello hug.

Out of puff we throw ourselves onto the seats on the carriage just as the doors glide shut.

"Hello my darling." Lacy says, breathing heavily, we both lean over the table between us and hug.

"I've missed you." I say holding her tight. You know that feeling when you haven't seen a friend in a while, but it still feels like no time has passed. That's what it's like with Lacy. Every time we're together it feels like we're kids again, we always end up doing something stupid that we would have done when we were young. I don't actually trust myself to go shopping with Lacy, because I know I'm going to end up buying a toy that I wanted when I was nine or completely reminisce over cartoon stationary, spend way too long in a book shop looking at rainbow fairy books. They were the best books ever to read. It made the readers feel special because the fairy had the same name as them. There was never an Ophelia rainbow fairy book, and that was something nine-year-old me couldn't understand, so I made up my own. 'Ophelia the awesome fairy' I named it, I wrote in the back of my maths notes, and I was very proud of it at the time.

Glasgow always scares me. It's so busy, I like to say that it's the New York of Scotland. Some people would argue that Edinburgh is the New York of Scotland. Glasgow is always busy, you can get food, tattoos and drugs at any time of day. And the streets have a very distinct smell of rubbish that after a few hours you get used to. It is over stimulating being here, the hustle and bustle drives me crazy, its giving very much, wolf of wall street vibes. And you know that some of these people are making money in a very sketchy, not legal way.

Lacy ushers me into Superdrug, where I do not need anything from, but I just happened to find things that I definitely need. The sales assistant sees me struggling and hands me a basket which only convinces me to fill it up with more stuff. The buy one get one half price is too good not to resist. "Hold on I need to pick up some condoms." Lucy whistles just as we're about to head to the tills. She browses the selection of condoms, flavoured, ribbed, mixed selection of sizes and colours. "I'm thinking of starting the pill, what kind of contraception do you and Blake use?" She asks picking up a blue box and tossing in her basket.

Oh um. Okay. It is strange that me and Blake have been dating for six months and we haven't had sex. It is a weird thing. I never realised it was this weird until Lacy just asked me what contraception I use and the fact that I don't have an answer. "Um. We haven't had sex yet." I admit, slurring my words to not draw any attention to me.

"What! You haven't had sex yet?" She shouts a little too loudly." "Sorry." She whispers. Edging towards me wanting me to spill.

Okay. Here I am. Telling people that don't really have any business knowing. In the middle of Superdrug. In the condom aisle. "Something happened to me. And I'm just not ready yet." I look at the floor. The words exhaust me like they always do.

"Ophelia. I am so sorry. I didn't know, I should never have reacted like that." Her arms warm me. "I'm so sorry that happened to you."

Anytime I tell someone about it it's like I'm back there again. "It's okay. I trust Blake now, so I don't know why I keep over thinking it, I want to have sex with Blake it's just that every time things heat up, I freak." *I definitely should not be having this conversation in a Superdrug. Definitely shouldn't.*

"You don't need to explain yourself to me. Come on let's go get a coffee." She rubs both hands against my forearms.

I nod. "Wait." I grab a box of condoms and chuck them into my basket. "I'm ready." I smile, wiping a tear that keeps trying to escape my eye.

I sit in the back of the coffee shop whilst Lacy orders our fancy drinks. I choose to sit in those extremely uncomfortably low chairs, with the table in front of them but you need to lean halfway over the table to drink because the seats are leaning back so far. You know the chairs that no one sits at. I wanted to be out of the way of everyone whilst I have this conversation.

"Okay. Talk to me." Lacy clanks our cups on the table and shakes her sugar packet.

I shake myself. "So Dans party. That's when it happened." Lacy's face trips when she puts the pieces together and goes back to that's night, collecting everything in her head like I've done a thousand times.

"Was it. Brian?"

I nod.

"Ophelia. I am so fucking sorry. I had no idea he was capable of that." She pulls her head down her knees.

"Lacy. Don't you dare apologise." I comfort her knee. "I have had to come to terms with a lot of things in the past seven months. And one of these things is that it was no one's fault but his." Taking a sip of my Carmel cinnamon latte. *Breathe.* "It's like every time me and Blake are together, I forget all about it, then when things get a bit touchy. I'm back there. It's not been that scary for a while. I trust Blake now. I just keep putting it off because subconsciously I think it'll happen again even though I know it won't." *I start rambling now.* "I mean, Blake would never do anything, and he's never made me think or feel like he would do something like that, so I just need to get over myself and have sex, but I want it to be special, so I don't want to rush into it. But oh fuck."

"Okay Ophelia. Breathe." Lacy looks up at me. *Breathe.* "If you think you're ready, go for it. But don't just do it because you think it's the right thing to do." She comforts my knee now. "I'm sorry that Brian done that to you." Her words are soft and sincere. "I just wish I knew earlier, and I would have been more sensitive with the subject."

"Lacy. Don't feel bad for that, only three people know. I didn't want to tell everyone I knew because then it would become a part of my personality and I don't feel like you should tell a lot of people because it's no one's business... I did want to tell you, because it is something that you tell your best friend, but it just never came up."

"I'm glad you told me Ophelia." She smiles comfortingly.

Back at home I unpack my bags. Why the fuck did I buy so much shit? I'm never going shopping with Lacy again. I take the plastic off the box of condoms. *I feel like a teenager, oh wait I am still a teenager, well a young teenager.* Holding a box of condoms that you bought feels like when you buy your first thong. I put them in my bedside drawer. I'm ready. I've realised that what happened with Brian, Blake isn't going to do. I just needed to talk it all out today. I missed having Lacy in my life. It's an important thing to have a close girl friend in your life, I never realised how important it was because I think I was dismissing the fact that it's okay to have girly chats and giggle about buying condoms or have gossip sessions in coffee shops about your sex life and not worry about the tables next to you over hearing. I like having a friend.

Chapter 14

My mum has her first ever training academy day today. I watched her late at night after doing an eleven-hour shift at the salon, then coming home to sit and study for hours to get her teaching certification. It was always her goal to have a training academy and be able to teach other budding beauty therapists the tricks of the trade. I had to design her branding and do all her marketing for it and also helped her decorate the academy. It's just the second floor of the salon. She had it set up as another treatment room but because it was up the stairs no one ever used it, so there she went swinging hammers into walls. She has worked so hard to be able to do this, I am so proud of her.

I haven't seen Blake all week because we've both been so busy at work. This is the last day we can spend together until college starts next week. We're going to have a movie day; our chosen movie genre is always Christmas. Even though its August its always time for a Christmas movie. Christmas was always a hard time for me. It still is sometimes. I've never had a family Christmas that I remember. Because even when my mum and dad were together, my mum didn't have a relationship with some of her family, so it was always really small. I like to imagine I'm in one of the families in one of the Christmas movies, who all dish up each other's food, pull Christmas crackers and play board games all night. It seems so nice.

I bring down blankets from the cupboard and fluff up all the pillows on the couch and make a little den. Movie days are our favourite thing to do, cuddling on the couch, eating our body weight in snacks and just being around each other.

Knock knock

I go to answer the door.

"Hello my love." Blake says, wrapping his arms around me, polly bag filled with snacks in hand. I take in his scent. He always smells so clean.

"Hello babes." I say, squishing my face into his chest. "I've missed you." You don't realise how much you miss being around someone until you're with them again and you get that surreal warmth in your chest.

"I missed you too." He looks down at me and I look up at him. Our lips touch tightly. I missed this.

We make our way over to the couch, Blakes shoes get kicked off and his jacket gets hung up on the coat stand in the hall. There's something so picturesque about cuddling. You're both so close yet not close enough. We know this movie by heart because we both grew up watching it but there's still some bits that make us laugh. My head is on Blake's chest and his hand tickles my shoulder. "Did you have a good day with Lacy yesterday?" He asks tucking my hair around the back of my neck.

"Yeah, it was so good. I got some things off my chest." I move my head, so my chin is on his chest.

He scrunches his eyebrows up, he always does that when he's worried, I don't think he notices he does it, but I do. "Everything okay?" Whispering softly, stroking my hair.

"Yeah... it's just." I take a deep breathe, smiling looking into his beautiful blue eyes. "I really trust you, Blake." I whisper, looking back and forth between his eyes and his mouth. I lean into him making our lips touch. He sits himself up and pulls me up with him, our hands on each other's faces. His tongue brushes against mine and everything just seems so right. It's like when I'm with Blake and we're kissing it's like the voices in my head that tell me I'm not good enough whisper sweet nothings. I trust Blake. I like Blake. I really like Blake. I straddle myself around his hips, he starts kissing down the length of my neck, holding onto my hips. I can feel him hard against me. "Do you want to have sex?" I ask moaning, smiling up at the ceiling.

He looks up at me. "Are you sure?" Stopping kissing me but wanting him to keep kissing me because I have him flustered.

"More than sure." Our lips are on each other's again. Breathing deeply to express how I feel. I want him, I want him in me. "Let's go up the stairs." I say between kisses. Blake throws the blanket from around me to the floor, gripping my legs around him whilst he stands up. My legs tighten around his waist. I let out a screech. He grins against my cheek.

 He gently places me on my bed, he rolls over onto my other side, continuing the kiss. Each kiss has more passion behind it, there's a purpose to each kiss now. One of his hands massage my hip whilst the other props himself up. I reach down and pull my top over my head. Blake looks me over, admiring me.

"You're so fucking beautiful Ophelia." He sighs, moving on top of me, his lips make their way down to my neck, I lean my head back giving him more surface area to kiss. Taking his time kissing me, like I'm a dessert and he's trying to savour every moment. He pulls his top off with one hand, smiling at me. His lips are on my chest now, his hands on the back of my thighs, pulling my thighs around his body. "Are you okay?" He asks.

"Yes Blake." I smile. I start tugging at my waistband of my trousers, Blake pulls away from kissing me and glides them off effortlessly. Showing off my matching lacey knickers. Blake bites his lip.

"Fuck me." He says under his breath.

"I'm trying to." I laugh, sitting up and unbuttoning his trousers for him. He laughs too, frantically removing his trousers, almost falling off the bed in the process. His boxers just low enough to see some stubbly hair. *Fuck, I'm due my wax next week.* "Blake." I laugh as he starts trailing kisses up my calves.

"You, okay?" He looks up at me with a look that's somewhat between glee and relaxation.

"Yeah." I chuckle. "I might be a but fluffy." I grin, biting my tongue.

"Ophelia. If you were a gorilla, I would still want to have sex with you." He grins, going back to kissing and caressing my thighs. *I never thought that I would find someone who would want to do all of this with me, let alone be willing to spend time with me. I never thought I'd find someone that I would want to do all this with. But here he is right in front of me.*

He plays with the waistband of my pants. "Stop teasing me." I say letting out a moan. Blake glides the knickers down. Tossing them into the growing pile of clothes at the side of my bed. Kissing my thighs again, Blake comes back up to my face and I start kissing his lips again.

"Shit." He sighs, putting his weight onto me. "I didn't bring a condom." *The worst thing that a guy can forget in this moment.* I twist around to my bedside table and pull of the box of condoms I bought yesterday. Smiling up at him. "You are fucking incredible Ophelia." Blake doesn't usually swear this much, there's just not enough words in the English language to explain how we feel right now. He pulls himself up, he sits on his knees. I sit up with him, pulling his boxers down to reveal himself. I kiss his chest whilst he tears open the condom wrapper with his teeth and rolls on the condom. We're back to kissing, my neck, my chest, my stomach. This is one of the very few times on my life where I've not felt self-conscious about my stomach. Is Blake cared about pudge at the bottom of my stomach he definitely would have walked away by now. Blakes hands make their way behind my back, touching my bra claps. "Are you sure this is okay Ophelia?" There's sorrow in his voice, like at any moment he thinks I'm going to ask him to stop.

I sigh and sit myself up. "Blake." I kiss his cheek. "I give you my one-hundred percent consent." I kiss his ear. "To do…whatever…the fuck…you want to me." I trail kisses down his neck. It takes Blake a second to realise what I've said. Then he tosses me down smiling, kissing he harder and more frantic. His lips slide down my breasts, my stomach, my hips, not parting with my skin before the next kiss is planted. His hands around my thighs, gripping them tight. His lips lusciously touch the inside of my legs and settle between my thighs.

Oh fuck.

Oh my.

Oh. My. Fuck.

My legs wrap themselves around Blake's shoulders to stop myself from screaming out his name. I really do hope that my mum doesn't come back from work early because she will definitely hear what's going on. I think I'll need to send my neighbours an apology basket because they can definitely hear everything that's happening right now.

My whole-body tenses, waves of pleasure ripple through me. My eyes roll farther back than they ever have before.

Then I let go.

Oh. My. Fuck.

I lie catching my breath, Blake's tongue moves up my body. I'm still groaning from joy. We start kissing again, more relaxed this time. "That was amazing." I gasp. Blake grins back at me. He looks at me and I know what he's asking. "Yeah." Blake thrusts himself into me gently. We both gasp. Our hands find each other's, our fingers tangled, and our bodies intertwined together. If I could tell myself from seven months ago that I would be able to enjoy being with someone so intimately without being scared she wouldn't believe me. I thought sex started and ended with hurt, fear and sadness. This isn't sex though. There's no way such a word can describe the beauty of this. This is making love. No matter how cheesy or cringey it sounds. There's a big difference between sex and making love. The asking of 'are you okay' every so often, the gentle kisses, the delicate hand holding, the soft moans coming from both parties, the staring into each other's eyes and knowing that there's no one else that you'd rather be doing this with. This is making love.

Afterwards, we lie, both still naked on my bed, a blanket draping over us, my head on his chest and we're still holding hands. There's nowhere else I'd rather be.

"Ophelia." Blake says. I turn my head up to him. "I love you." My heart fills when he says it.

"I love you too." I say back. I think I want to start saying that more often.

Chapter 15

I've been floating on a cloud the past few days. The next morning when Blake left, we said we loved each other again. I don't think I'll get over that warm blanket that covers your heart when you say it. If I could just stay in my little bubble of joy and cosiness I'd be over the moon. But I start college today. Mine and Blakes schedules are pretty much the same so we go can go into college together and leave college together. If I'm being honest with myself, I don't want to go to college. I do but I don't. I'm looking forward to the routine and the college lifestyle, even though it's not going to be like the American movies with frat parties and beer pong, I like to think that it is though.

Blake runs around to the passenger side of the car to open the door for me. I smile appreciating it. it's the little things like that, that make me feel loved. I look at Blake and grin, saying thank you with my eyes. It's not fair, the beauty therapy students need to wear all black, tunics and flat shoes, no trainers, hair scraped back in a bun. I've tried to put my own little spin on the uniform though, I've got my hair in a low bun with my baby hairs down and curly and of course a few glittery clips to jazz it up. In the barbering course that Blake is doing all the dress code says is to be dressed in all black, not fair. I guess that's just another way that misogyny brings young women down.

In the reception area of the college, lecturers gather the different classes and me and Blake are separated. When I walk into my first class it's exactly like school. I feel trapped, like a fish in a fishbowl. There are the pretty girls dollying themselves up like peacocks, then there's me. I've always been the odd one out, the ugly duckling of the class. Even in primary school, I would wear my hair in hairstyles that none of the other girls had, I loved how I had my hair in pigtails with colourful clips, because that's who I am, but the other girls would have their hair down, with straight cut fringes that I used to be very jealous of. *Very glad I didn't have a fringe now looking back on it.* I go to the front of the class and sit by myself.

Everyone hates me already. They found out that my mum has a salon and think I'm a snob. I mean, they all have no idea what they're doing, and I already know most of the stuff that we've went over. I want to skip this stage of my life. What they don't tell you about growing up is that once you leave high school, the part of your life that is structured and you are told what to do you have no idea how to act once you're not there anymore. A part of you still wants to be he girl that raises her hand and doesn't speak unless spoken to and then there's the real you that wants to speak up and tell people that they are idiots. I want to skip this awkward stage and go straight to being a boss bitch adult woman.

I'm working until late tonight, so is Blake. It's Tuesday night so it's my in the salon night.

"How was your first day?" Blake asks, trotting up to me in the reception area. I have been standing waiting on him for five minutes. His new kit bag full of hair tools on his shoulder. His arms wrap around me. I've wanted this hug all day, my face pressed against his chest, warm and safe.

"It was good." I don't know why I lied. I hide the fact that I'm close to tears from disappointment, but I think I'm more disappointed in myself.

Blake drops me off outside of the salon, looking over at the neon sign in the window I put my happy face on. One of the hardest parts about working at a beauty salon is that your job is making people feel good about themselves so if you don't feel good about yourself, you can't do your job. I must be terrible at my job most of the time. Blakes soft lips kiss my cheek before I leave his car. "I love you." He says.

There it is the warmth and cosiness. "I love you too." The words put a smile on my face and I'm ready for work. I wave Blake away, shaking the day off of me. My mum's salon is always busy, she's the best in the business, all her girls are amazing at their jobs. Everyone waves at me when I go in, the top hits playing full blast throughout the salon, the smell of vanilla and acetone trickle their way down the corridor to the kitchen.

"Hi Ophelia, how was your first day?" Mum asks, sipping her coffee. When you work in a salon you survive on coffee, tea and biscuits, it's the rules.

I think about my answer for a second. Do I want to lie? I don't want my mum to be disappointed, she wouldn't be disappointed at me. "I didn't like it." I didn't lie, I'm proud of myself. "Sorry." Tilting my head back, closing my eyes tight.

"Don't be sorry. If you didn't like it, that okay." She gets up from her chair, her words muffled by biscuits. Giving me a hug from the side. "You don't need to do it if you don't want to." Her words bring me comfort. I applied for this course in January, its August. In January I wanted to be a full-time beauty therapist and glam people up all day every day. Now I just want to work behind the scenes and be more present online. I don't want to deal with clients all day. After working for my mum for most of my life I've met some arsehole people. Some clients think your life starts and ends in the salon, and I don't want to get to the point that I believe that's true. Remember in school, when you'd see your teachers in the supermarket and it would be like a strange crossover episode, because you didn't realise that your teachers had a life outside of school. Well, that's what sone clients think. My mum has had a regular client ask her to do her eyebrows at eight on a Sunday morning before. She wasn't a regular client for long after that. I want to be able to make my own working hours and have long lies in the morning and take my laptop to coffee shops and work whilst having creamy and overpriced hot chocolate. I want to have a romantic life and enjoy the little moments when I'm myself, instead of coming home from an eleven-hour shift and quickly getting into bed, ready to do it all again in the morning. I don't want to end up like my mum.

Once I start work, it's not so bad, I answered messages and edited content for social media, scheduled posts for Instagram. The hours went by pretty fast, but there's nothing I want more right now than a shower and my bed. Realising that the career that you have dedicated so many years to isn't for you, really requires a prescription of a shower and a comfy bed.

Dear diary,

I feel like sometimes the world is spinning and I can feel it. The world travels at three hundred and sixty miles per hour and you don't feel it, but I can. Apart from now. I'm washed and alone. That's the only time I feel steady. The world goes too fast. When I'm around people and out in the public there's so many things going on at once and it's hard to keep track of what I'm doing, like I'm holding sand and all the granules are slipping out between my fingers and I can't keep them in my hands.

I've had a shitty day. I'm not going back to college tomorrow. I don't like it. I don't want to be guilty about not liking it. I've had a day where no matter what I done, I felt like I done it wrong, I didn't do anything wrong but I feel like I have; I could have made a better first impression at college and maybe I wouldn't hate it, I could have replied to the idiot nicer and maybe they would have booked in, I could have held the door open for one more person when I went to the shop and that's why no one said thank you. It's a constant battle in my head that I could have done something better and been a nicer person. It's exhausting. There's only thing that I want to do right now. Blake.

Love Lia

Xox

Ring ring

"Hi Blake." I grin, answering the call. We are genuinely telepathic sometimes, it's scary.

"Hi Ophelia. I have just finished work, do you want to go out for a drive?" He asks, already knowing my answer. "I'll pick you up in ten minutes."

Leaping off my bed, throwing on a cute black bra and a top that isn't pyjamas. Before Blake, I would have never wanted to go out after nine o'clock, my rule was always 'once my blinds are shut so is my door.' Blake urges me to go out and do things, he adds extra hours onto my day, and I don't feel nearly as exhausted. Mum is in the living room with a pint of ice cream and freshly made popcorn, watching one of her five comfort movies, which means she's had a bad day too. "Mum I'm going out with Blake, I love you." I creep past the living room; she one hundred percent did not hear me.

"I love you." She says, engrossed in her movie shoving handfuls of popcorn into her mouth.

Standing in the driveway waiting for Blake, like I used to wait for my dad. I don't like thinking about him. At least Blake shows up. Smiling and happy to see me. Receiving the princess treatment as always as me opens the door for me. Waiting to start the car until he knows that I'm okay and my seatbelt is secure.

The music is quiet, and my heart is at peace because Blakes hand in on me, softly touching my thigh in between changing gears. We drive to our space, that's what we've started calling it, it's the car park that we went to on our first date, we've went once a week since we started seeing each other. And we've never seen another person there, so we like to think that its only us that know about it. It overlooks a field and it's surrounded by trees so you can't see it until your actually there.

Our seatbelts and shoes are off. My feet are crossed over the seats and on Blake's knees.

"I've really missed you." I speak. We've been silent for most of the journey.

"You saw me six hours ago." He smiles. "I missed you too." His eyes trace me. "I really want to kiss you right now." Whispering under his breathe, undressing me in his mind.

Leaning over to him slowly, my hand on his face, just before our lips lock, I pull away and cheese, he does the same thing. I straddle myself over Blake, his lips taking me in, I've wanted this all day, his hands grab my hips, pushing his hips up to meet mine, pulling mine closer to him, our lips travel across each other faces, each of us letting out whimpers.

"Do you want to have sex?" Blake asks, his lips on my neck.

"Please." I beg. I've had a hard day and all I want is Blake inside of me. I drag my top off my body revealing my black bra, throwing my top into the back seat, Blakes mouth is on my chest, his hands are on my waist. Our kisses become quicker and have more thirst. Our lips are firm against each other's. Blake pulls his top off and tosses it next to mine in the back seat. Jumping over to the passenger seat I quickly tug my trousers and knickers off, Blake unbuttons his jeans and shimmies them down. "I've never had sex in a car before." I laugh, trying to untangle my knickers from my trousers.

Blake looks at me up and down and laughs. "I hope you don't think I expected this." He reaches over to the glove box and pulls out a strip of condoms." He tears a one of them off of the strip and opens it.

"Blake. I really don't give a shit. I want you to fuck me." My clothes get catapulted into the back seat as I move over back to Blake's lap, straddling him again, hovering over his hips. Our lips are together again, I use Blake's neck for balance, looking down adjusting myself, he takes my hips and slowly lowers me onto him, we both take a deep inhale, moaning as we do so. I grind myself back and forth, Blake's hip move with me. Blake hands move down.

Oh fuck.

His hands are right where I want them, right where I like it.

"Are you okay?" Blake asks between his deep groans, gripping my thigh and still touching me.

"Yes." My nails scratch at Blake's shoulders, tightening themselves with every wave. It's those little check ins, even when we're kissing. Blake does so many little things that he probably doesn't even think twice about, but they mean so much to me. They mean that he respects me and wants me to feel appreciated and safe. We keep going, moving back and forth, up and down until it all becomes one big eruption. We finish. *I finished twice.* Our kissing slows down, I'm still on top of him and he's still inside of me.

"You're really beautiful Ophelia." He trembles, tucking my hair behind my ear.

"I feel really beautiful when I'm with you Blake." My hand strokes his face. "You're really beautiful too." I never thought that you could consider men beautiful, I would always be handsome, hot, sexy. But there are endless things about Blake that are beautiful, his soul is so incredibly pure, and he does everything with the intention of it helping someone else. Blake is so incredibly beautiful.

"I feel really beautiful when I'm with you too Ophelia." His thumb grabs across my cheek, kissing me again.

We take our time in getting dressed again. Having clothes against us when we are around each other feels unnatural, I would quite happily spend eternity in this car, in this car park, naked with Blake. We sit in silence for while whilst the windows de fog themselves and while the sky gets darker, and the moon gets brighter. We still haven't got fully dressed, his jeans are still unbuttoned, and my shoes aren't tied. I feel happy now.

Chapter 16

Dear diary,

I handed in my college dropout email. As hilarious as it sounds, I am a beauty school dropout. Really just living my Frenchie from grease fantasy. I'm the happiest I've felt in a while. I get up in the morning, make a cute breakfast and work on the couch. I've ended up with a pretty big following on social media which has come with its perks. Brands are reaching out to me and offering me money. Like money money, to post about them. Most of them are beauty brands, skincare, tan etc. I never would have thought that me, a chunky weird girl would have brands reaching out to me. I'm still working for my mum, part time though. Which is great. But I do sometimes feel like it's a pity job. I am planning on releasing something soon. I've always wanted to have my own brand. It's always been a dream of mine. As a little girl I wanted to own my own shop and that might still happen. I've looked into apparel and accessories, and I've became obsessed. I've designed some decals for them. The one thing I loved about beauty was making people feel good about themselves, I want to do that through other things. It will be a huge investment for me, especially since I'm trying to learn to drive and driving lessons are not cheap, but it will be worth it in the end. Hopefully. No, I need to stop doubting myself. It will be successful.

I've not told anyone about my plans, not even Blake, or my mum. My mum has grown suspicious though, an awful

*lot of parcels arriving. More than usual anyways. I've
been spending my nights staying up and doing everything
in secret which includes buying tools and equipment.
Whoops. I don't know why I haven't been telling people
about it. I guess I'm just afraid that it is not going to work
out and it will be a waste of money, and everyone will
laugh at me. I know that no one is going to laugh at me or
make this a big, massive joke but that's where my mind
immediately goes when I make decisions like this. I've
been chatting to a printing company that wants to print my
products that I've designed. But I do not think that I can
keep one thousand t shirts and hoodies and tote bags a
secret. The spare bedroom might just need to become a
warehouse for a few months, until I move out.*

*Blake keeps mentioning that he wants to move in together
when he leaves college. I can't think of anything I'd hate
more. It's not that I don't want to be with Blake. I do. I
just don't want to live with him. I can't live with him
without living by myself. I don't want to turn our
relationship into my mum and dads. I'm sick of comparing
everything to my mum and dad but I can't help it. It would
just be too much for me and Blake to move in together, for
me anyway. If Blake had it his way, we would have moved
in together already and we would be engaged, and our
world would start and end with each other. And that is
much too much commitment for me. I can't even commit to
watching a new tv show.*

*I'm getting excited about my secret project though. I will
tell my mum, tonight, before my shipment of products
come next week. I'll post it on my social media as well,
then it will become so real and scary. I have the day all to
myself today and I have the house to myself as well.
Everyone I know is at college, university or work, which*

only means one thing. Lazy day where I read books and watch movies. I haven't been reading as much, which isn't good for me. I've always been someone who goes through a book a week kind of thing but I've just not enough time to read more than a chapter every few days. Let's become a boss bitch. And maybe finally get our life together.

Love Lia

Xox

Chapter 17

Three weeks later

My brand is launching tonight, I did finally tell my mum and she was so supportive, and Blake was just as happy when he found out. Okay he was a little pissed off that I didn't tell him sooner. I just wanted this to be *my* thing. For so long people compared me to my mum because I wanted to be just like her. And I wanted something that no one would pick apart or be involved in. It's just me.

I have spent weeks perfecting designs, creating a website and picking out the perfect packing supplies. It is my birthday tomorrow, which is why I wanted to launch the website tonight. I hate my birthday. But it's my eighteenth so I should be looking forward to it. My birthdays in the past I've been at school, or I would be at home alone. My mum would set my gifts out and have a balloon waiting for me waking up. And as much as I appreciated it, it just reminded me of how lonely I was. This is my first birthday where I have people to spend it with. I have Blake, Dan and Lacy. Although I don't want fuss.

Admiring my mini warehouse in the spare room, I built shelving units that completely cover a whole wall filled with t shirts, hoodies and tote bags all with amazing quotes…

'Sprinkle kindness around like confetti'

'Know your worth, then add tax'

and my personal favourite- 'rich by 30'

I can't wait until it all goes well, and I can move into my own place and can have an actual office space to store more stuff and products, I'm already planning more launches. This is something I am extremely passionate about.

"T minus two hours." Blake sings, sneaking up behind me. "I'm proud of you." His arm wraps around my waist. Those words are a symphony, singing in harmony. He doesn't realise how amazing those words sound. Especially when he says them, and especially when they're said to me. No matter how my launch goes I need to remain proud of myself. When I announced it all of my followers were extremely supportive, my mum has set up a little stall in the salon with a clothing rail and has not stopped speaking about it with clients since I told her.

Sitting in front of my laptop as the countdown begins.

10. 9. 8. 7. 6. 5. 4. 3. 2. 1.

The screen lights up with confetti, I post a picture on Instagram to commemorate the moment. I can see a few people on my site already!

Ping

My first order is in.

Ping *Ping*

Oh my god. Three orders in my first minute.

This is going to be good.

I sit myself, watching the order count go up. I can hear mum and Blake chatting in the living room. But I don't want to join in the conversation, I just want to sit right here and be present in the moment. Twenty orders. People actually want to buy something that I designed and worked hard on? My Instagram notifications are blowing up with people tagging me in their order confirmations and people reposting my profile and website. Self Care Co is my life now.

Knock knock

The lights dim.

"Happy birthday to you, happy birthday to you, happy birthday to Ophelia, happy birthday to you!" Blake and mum sing, smiling with their stupid big grins. I hold my head in my hands, cringing. I've always hated my birthday. Since I was about nine anyways. When you grow up, your birthday isn't an exciting thing anymore. you don't get to circle toys on the Argos catalogue. Your birthday is a reminder that you're growing up, something that you wanted to do so much when you were a child but as the years go on you want to be little again. The glorious birthday cake is in front of me, with a big '18' candle in the middle. I blow it out and they applaud. The last thing on my mind right now is my birthday, I want to sit and watch my website and package orders and run a company, maybe with a slice of birthday cake to keep me company.

I stay up all night. The house is quiet. Blake went home and my mum is asleep. There's a lot of things about 4am that bring me peace. No one is awake. Chances are anyway. If you look out the windows, you're not going to see anyone, there won't be cars on the roads, there won't be kids causing trouble. It's just you.

Chapter 18

Tonight, is Dans graduation party. It's his first party since what happened to me. Anyone who was invited went through a 'trust test'. And he has made sure that everyone that is bringing a friend is a good person. *A fucking bouncer for a graduation party.* Dan didn't think he was going to graduate high school. I think he got a bit of a reality check this past year, he saw Lacy go off to university and he saw me make massive decisions for my career. He got a conditional offer to Glasgow university to study law, to be just like his mum. I'm proud of him. When I first met him and up until a year ago, he was always the class clown, handed in homework late, if at all, he has worked extremely hard this year to get his grades up. Now it's just a waiting game to see if he got his A and two Bs that he needs to get in.

I get my sparkly pink dress that I bought for this occasion out of my wardrobe and slide it onto my freshly moisturised body, staring in the full-length mirror at myself.

"Ophelia are you ready?" Blake knocks on the door whilst he opens it. "You look beautiful." He closes the door behind him.

"You don't scrub up too bad yourself." I spin round to face him, admiring his black silky shirt. "Can you zip me up." I look up at him.

He plays with his tongue in his mouth and nods. Taking his hand to my hip and spinning me around, pressing his hand against the small of my back, twiddling the zipper. His touch makes me play back memories in my head. I throw my head back to his. He slowly pulls the zipper up, his breath on my neck the entire time. His hand spins me back round to face him. We're kissing now. Kissing is our default mode in most things. We don't know what to say? We kiss. We're annoyed? We kiss. We're horny? We kiss. It's our natural state for our lips to be together. We kiss a lot.

By the time our lip's part we are running late for the party. We walk, arms looped, my other hand gripping onto Blake. I'm safe now, I don't need to worry about going to Dans house, or Dans party, but still, being there, I'm afraid it will bring up past issues. We walk down to the shop; I hate this town. Everyone knows me as my mum's daughter. My mum grew up here as well, no matter where I go its 'oh I know your mum'. I want to move from the safety and security from here. Blake wants to stay here though. In the shop Blake goes for the classy, sexy drink of whiskey. I opt for the less classy, scheme wean litre of vodka. Flashing my ID to the sales assistant that has been selling me alcohol since I was fifteen. They know my mum, so they trusted me. At least I wasn't getting drunk and getting fingered in fields like half of my school. I was sophisticated and got drink alone in the safety of my house. I haven't drunk for a few months; I might have actually been just after my eighteenth birthday when I had a few cocktails in the house. Clubs, pubs and bars aren't my scene.

I can feel the nerves build up in my chest when we reach Dans driveway. Letting out a deep breath, shaking myself. "Are you okay?" Blake whispers as he reaches for the door handle.

I nod. "I just need a drink." I let out another deep breath, still gripping onto Blake's arm.

The door opens and it's a swarm of loudness and people. "It's okay." Blake squeezes me. We make our way through the living room, which is more like and ocean and try and get past the waves of people. Everyone is looking at me. Apparently, I've made a name for myself. According to Dan, I'm the new school gossip. I have girls waving at me like they didn't ignore me for years. Walking past the couch. Where Brian was sitting. This was a bad idea. But I want to be here for Dan. Plus, Lacy will be here soon, and I haven't seen her in a few weeks. Blake takes me to the safety of the kitchen; the back door is open, and I can smell the second-hand smoke wafting its way thought the house.

Blake hands me a glass whilst he fills his glass with whiskey and a few ice cubes. I pour my vodka into the glass, adding an ice cube for balance.

"Cheers." I say clinking our glasses together, gulping down the entire glass. Exhaling sharply to heal the burn.

Blake raises his eyebrows, taking a sip of his whiskey. "Take it easy."

There's a part of me that wants to shout at him and tell him not to tell me what to do, but he's right, I choose to not listen, pouring myself a second glass. "I just need to blow of some steam." Feeling the tears built up in my eyes. Biting the inside of my lip to stop me from bawling my eyes out as the memories from a year and a half ago play back in my mind.

"Okay." Blake finishes his drink, slamming the glass on to the worktop, clenching his jaw as his throat rolls.

Why does everyone here get to be okay? Why do they get to be okay about being here? I'm not okay about being here. Staring at the indent on the couch and wondering if Brian is here. I know he's not but what if he is? What if he's waiting for me up the stairs? What if I see him? Am I supposed to act like nothing happened to me? It's been over a year, but I'm still scared, I still think about it all the time. I've thought about it all day today because I knew I'd feel like this tonight. I can feel myself going into overdrive as I finish my third glass of straight vodka. I don't like drinking. I don't like how I feel when I've had a drink. I used to drink because it gave me a nice buzz and made me forget things and be happy. Now it just reminds me of bad things. Blake has been avoiding me for the past twenty minutes. He is staying close by though. Lacy got here and is introducing herself to Dans classmates that she's never met. That's something about Lacy that makes me extremely jealous, she can talk to literally anyone, about anything. A group of girls has surrounded me, they are reminiscing on high school, any happy memory they bring up I can think of a hundred reasons why it's not a happy memory. Like when in home economics when we set the fire alarm off baking scones, and it was hilarious because we all had to go out into the pitch and wait for the fire brigade to clear the area. I had spent the night before sad and alone and thinking about Brian. And I hadn't slept, and I forgot to set the oven timer and I burned the scones which set the alarm off, and everyone laughed at me. Not with me. At me. That was two weeks after I was raped. Or when they ask me how my relationship with Blake is, I know that they mean; that I'm not good enough for him, I'm not skinny enough, not pretty enough, not perfect enough. Everyone from school makes me feel like I have a black cloud hovering over me and makes me feel like I'm dragging everyone down.

"The last time I was at one of Dans parties I was raped." I pipe up, interrupting them. They turn to look at me. "Yeah. I don't know who I am anymore because of it. I didn't realise how much it affected me, but it does, even now over a year later it still affects me. As much as I don't want it to affect me it does." Blake rushers over, overhearing me. "Oh, my darling Blake. You have done so much for me, even though we didn't have sex for six months you stuck by me." I latch my arms around his neck.

"Come on, it's okay." He pulls me up.

Dan comes over as well, a wall of people starts building around me. "Dan oh my god. I love you so much, even though we only became proper friend when you other friends left school, I appreciate you so much."

"Okay Lia, you've had too much to drink let's get you to bed." I have no idea what he's talking about I've only had three drinks. They were pretty big drinks. Everyone's eyes are on me again. I hate it.

These stairs bring back bad memories. I never realised how much I remembered from that night until I came back here. I never thought that the stairs would play a big part of the story, but they do, they led me to the worst night of my life, and I should have never gone up them. I want nothing more right now than to leave. Leave this party, leave this town and reinvent myself. But I can't stop thinking about how good Blake smells right now and how well his shirt fits him.

I'm sitting on the edge of Dans mum's bed. Staring at Blake as he kneels, sliding my shoes off me, he is so perfect, and I don't deserve him. Not one bit.

"You're too good for me Blake." I say as he gets up from my knees. He doesn't say anything. "I really want to kiss you." Standing up to his level. Our lips are back in default mode, together, kissing. The taste of his Jack Daniels on his breath coats my tongue, my hands are in his hair, pushing his face closer to mine. Blakes hands are on my body, everywhere on my body, my waist, my hair, my hips. His hands are exactly where I want them. Blake leans himself onto the bed, not letting our lip's part, pulling my legs over him, kissing him, I can't stop thinking about how much I want to kiss him all the time. I throw us back so I'm fully on top of Blake, I start grinding my hips against his, watching him squirm, our lips still together. Sitting up, pulling my dress straps down over my bra.

"Ophelia. I don't think now is a good time to have sex." Blake says. His words are hurtful. He sees the hurt on my face, propping himself up with his hands, I'm still on top of him. "You've been drinking. And I don't think here is the right place." He pulls my dress straps back up my shoulders. Tucking my hair out of my face.

I'm so fucking embarrassed. And annoyed. And sad. And angry. And horny.

Rolling off of him, facing the window, sniffing the tears back into my eyes. "Ophelia. I love you. You've not been yourself all night, and I don't want to have sex with you unless you're okay." His hand traces my upper arm. "Are you okay."

Of course, I'm not okay. My fucking boyfriend doesn't want to have sex with me because I'm not acting happy and cheery. Why the fuck would I be acting happy and cheery? I'm in the house that I was fucking raped in. I'm in the house that I was in when my life was ruined.

"I'm okay." I lie.

I need to stop doing that. Lying about my feelings when I'm obviously lying. I know that if I say to Blake that I'm not okay and need a hug, Blake will hug me and talk to be to make me feel better. I just don't want to put my issues onto someone else. I don't want to let go. I don't want to trust someone else with what goes on in my head. I don't trust myself right now and I can't help but love how Blake is reacting to this. He is laying behind me, with his arm around me and his other arm stroking my hair. I can feel the party still going on underneath me. At least I didn't wreck this party this time.

It's the next morning. I didn't sleep much. I kept tossing and turning. Thinking. About how I can't do this. I can't keep lying to myself. I got myself up and ready before Blake woke up.

Raiding the junk drawer in the kitchen to find painkillers to soothe this banging headache. I didn't drink that much. I don't think I did anyway. I know I made a fool of myself last night. I know I did. But I don't get how people can act like everything's okay and that everything is normal. All of a sudden everyone has become an adult, and everyone is supposed to be moving on with their lives, but I'm stuck where I've always been. I'm not happy. I feel like I'm thirteen again, being bullied and I hate myself again. Why does everyone get to move on, and I can't?

Blake wakes up and I ignore him. I'm not annoyed at him, or angry. I just can't deal with being around him today. He is suffocating me. He is taking care of me, and I don't like it. For once in my life, I don't want someone to hold my hand through everything. I don't know who I am anymore. My identity starts and ends as Blake's girlfriend. I don't look at myself and see Ophelia, I see Blake's girlfriend. I don't want to be Blake's girlfriend anymore.

Chapter 19

I hate myself. I've become a monster. Dans graduation party was enough for me to realise. I don't know who I am anymore. And I hate it.

I've became exactly who I said I wouldn't become. My mother. She lost herself slowly for fourteen years. I don't want to lose myself like she did. I can't stay here anymore. I can't be in a relationship anymore. Blake wants us to have a life together. A house, a family. I don't want any of that. I love Blake, but I don't love him like that. I don't want to give up on my dreams to settle down. Blake wants to take care of me and wants me to be safe. I don't want to be safe anymore. I don't want to be taken care of. I want to look after myself, be self-sufficient. Take risks, take risks in my appearance, my career, risks I might regret, but I might not regret them. I don't want to be safe anymore. moving out of this shitty small town that made Blake feel safe might be the thing that sets me free. Blake might hate me for it. I hope he doesn't hate me though. Blake has done so much for me over the last year and a half-ish. He has shown me what love is, I don't know if I can love someone like Blake loves someone, your whole world starts and ends with them.

Blake jogs into the kitchen. I've been standing in front of these potatoes for ten minutes, staring into the abyss thinking about how I don't want this. I don't want to live with Blake. And how he wants to live with me. And I don't want to be making his fucking potatoes for his fucking dinner. I don't want to love someone just because they love me. I don't want to love someone when I fucking hate myself.

"Blake." He keeps yammering on about a flat that he has seen. "Blake!" I say louder. He looks up at me, his eyes are sad. "I can't do this anymore." It feels like a weight has been lifted off my shoulders. Like I can finally breathe again,

"What?" He drops his phone on the kitchen island, I'm still standing in front of the potatoes.

"I can't love you anymore." My attention away from the potatoes and on Blake. His distraught eyes become closer to mine; he rushes over to me behind the island.

"Ophelia. What's wrong? Have I done something?" He turns me around to him by the elbows.

How I wish he would have done something. I wish that he would have been cheating on me so I can give a reasonable explanation as to why I can't do this anymore. "I can't love you anymore… because. I don't love myself anymore." My eyes meet his. My blank expression turns sour. Blake grips me at the waist.

"No Ophelia. Don't say that. I can't not love you anymore. It's okay. I can fix this. I can help you." He bubbles. I want to say 'you only want to be with me because I remind you of your mum and you want to help her' but that's nasty. It's true. But its nasty.

"Blake, stop it." I sigh, brushing his hands off of me. The tears start to well up in my eyes. "You deserve so much better. You deserve to be with someone who can love you as much as you love them… and as much as I want to love you. I can't give you all the things you desire."

"Ophelia. I just want you." Blake grabs my face gently but still with power. "I just want to be with you. I've never felt the way that I do with you with anyone. I just want to be with you forever."

That's what scares me. "Blake. I love you so much. And that's why I'm doing this. I can't promise forever with you. I can't promise that in six months' time I'll be ready to move in together. I can't promise you a wedding or kids… I am holding you back from what you want. And you deserve someone who wants to have all those things with you and doesn't need to think about it."

Blake sits his head on my shoulder, and I do everything in my power not to fall in love with him all over again. Wrapping my arms around his shoulders as we both cry into each other's clothes. "I love you, Ophelia." He speaks. My face trembles.

"I love you too Blake." Tears trickle down my face.

He leaves. Without looking at me, he leaves, he picks his face up from my body, turns around and shuts the front door behind him. I watch out the window as his blue Corsa pulls out of the driveway. I love him. But that's why I'm doing this. I can't drag Blake down. So, I'm letting him go. I'm looking back at the potatoes now. I look at the potatoes for a while. The sky goes dark as the sun sets. There's a poem I read, I really need to stop reading poetry because they ruin me but this is how it goes…

I killed a plant once

Because I gave it to much water

I worry that love is violence

-Jose Olivarez

I think the poem is true. Love is violence. It always hurts in the end. And if you love something too much you're going to hurt it.

My mum announces to the house that she is home from work before she notices me in the kitchen. "Hi darling. Are you okay?" She asks. I'm still standing staring at the potatoes.

"No. I'm not okay." I didn't lie this time. That's the first time in a long time that I haven't lied to make other people happy. "I broke up with Blake. And I'm moving." Mum doesn't say anything she just dumps her bag and rushes to me, wrapping her arms around me. Around where Blake was. To think that the number of times that Blake hugged me, I never appreciated it as much as I should have. Or I would have made the last time we hugged before today last longer and I would have taken more notes on which shower gel he used that morning or what aftershave he had on, or I would have noticed if his heart raced a bit more or if he kept a hand on me after the hug ended. I wish I could hug him one last time. "I need out of this place."

"I know you do." She admits.

This place isn't good for me. Too many things have happened. There are too many people here that know too much about me. They know who my mum is, they know my mum's family more than I do, more than my mum does. They know all about my dad's new family. They know things about me that I don't know. Everyone has an idea of who I am, I'm a beauty therapists' daughter. No one knows Ophelia Opal Bloom. I don't. I'm doing it. I'm moving out of this crappy town, the town that broke me.

Moving away from running into ex-friends at the supermarket, seeing your bullies cross the street, moving away from the constant reminder that I am nothing like everyone else in this town. Moving away from the old me. The me that secretly hates who she's become no matter how much she lies to those around her. She hates that when she looks in the mirror, she gets reminder of her dad and the fact that he hasn't picked up the phone in over a year, the reminder that she was friends with shitty people because she was so desperate for attention. The reminder that she was raped, and she hasn't been the same since. I don't know who that person is in the mirror. But I hate her. The person that tries to please others and hurts herself in the process. That person who behind that shiny exterior is broken inside. She's been broken for a while. I want to fix her.

For the first time in my life. I choose me.

Chapter 20

Dear diary

It's been two months since I broke up with Blake. I've thought about him a lot. I didn't leave the house for a week. I couldn't. I'm feeling better now. I went a little manic. I spur of the moment booked a driving test. I passed. Which is insane considering I only done ten lessons and scraped by with my theory test. I'm still looking for a car though. I found an apartment. Mind blowing. I move in next week. I haven't packed because everything has gone by so fast.

A list of things that have happened in the past two months…

- *I broke up with Blake and broke his heart.*
- *I passed my theory test.*
- *My company Self Care Co has blown up online and I'm selling out with every restock.*
- *I passed my driving test.*
- *I have an apartment that I'm moving into.*
- *I went to the doctors for help with my mental health. I'm being referred to a therapist. And I got put on anti-anxiety and antidepressants. Which I'm supposed to go between.*

It was horrifying for me to finally reach out for help with my mental health. I've always struggled, ever since I was a child. Sometimes I just can't sort myself out. I've never been able to relax I've always been 'high' but then I get low lows. It was my mum that asked me to go. She's been on medication for her mental health since she was fourteen. They do say that mental health is genetic. My gene pool is top tier if you ask me. That was sarcastic if you can't tell. I'm not focused on a relationship anymore. I'm trying to better myself which is something that I never quite fully understood until I came out of a relationship. I became obsessed with everything, how would Blake like this? How would Blake like that? That isn't healthy. I should have been thinking how do I feel about this? No one else's opinion matters but your own. 'Love yourself first' it has been plastered over the house since I was a baby, but I never understood it. I think it means that you can't full give yourself to someone until you know yourself fully first, and accept every single part of you, the good and the bad.

For the past two months I've been going in and out of the post office with parcels which is insane to me, that someone, thousands of people actually want to purchase things that I have designed. In my new apartment I'm not going to have a living room, not really anyway, it's only a one bedroom so I don't have the extra space for all of my stock or my desk, but I'm going to try and somehow divide the living room so its half office half couch? I'll figure it out when I move in, I've planned out my future home in my head millions of times and how I want it to look and every time it's something different. I'll see what happens when I get there.

When I spur of the moment booked my driving test I was freaking out because I had only done ten lessons, so I did not expect to pass, but I'm so glad that I took the chance. The person who was doing the test with me definitely should one-hundred percent not have passed me. I am a terrible driver. I'm going to need a car before I move so that's another thing on my never ending to do list. I've been trying to keep myself busy since I broke up with Blake. I think about him a lot if I'm honest with myself. I don't let myself believe I think about him, I push him to the back of my head, but he's still there. Dan told me that he's dating someone else. Which breaks my heart. It shouldn't, but it does. I need to get over it. I need to look at bigger and better things, I'm fucking moving, and buying a car. I have a big girl, adult job. I'm a grown up now. That's scary. One minute I was a high school student studying for her exams and the next I'm a full-grown adult moving on with her life and making a life for herself. I wish adulting class for a part of school. Like how do you pay bills? How do you set everything up to pay bills? How do you buy a car? Let's hope I figure all of that out by next week.

Love Lia

xox

Taping up boxes of everything I own feels like I'm being shipped off halfway around the world, when I'm really just going thirty minutes away. Still, it doesn't take away how huge this is for me. My mum put together a little starter kit for moving, she got me a tool kit for building my furniture, cleaning sprays, towels and a key ring that has a heart on it. I don't leave until tomorrow, but I also leave tomorrow! I have so much still to pack. I have my entire business to pack. I purposefully didn't order stock this month because I knew there would be no point in unpacking it all to them pack it all to then unpack it all all over again.

As much as I love this house, it's my home, it's been my home for almost nineteen years. I am glad as hell to get out of it. Everything is too comfortable, and I know that if anyone asked my mum, she wouldn't want me to leave, I think that's why she hasn't been helping me pack, she's just pretending that its not going to happen and blocking it out, even when I move out, she'll still pretend that I live here, not do anything with my bedroom because its my room still. This house will be my inheritance, when I'm sixty and retired I'll live here, me and the neighbours will be best friends and crochet blankets together and share recipes, but that's forty years from now. The world could have ended by then. So, for the next forty years I need to be the best version of myself and become the person I want to tell people about when I'm sixty, the person to gloat about to all of my pensioner friends. Hopefully I can still be that person when I'm sixty.

Chapter 21

Its right now, slamming my own car door shut, that I drove here, here being my new flat, that I pay for by myself that I realise. I never thought that I would have accomplished any of that. I did it. I moved into my own apartment. In Glasgow of all places. I stand at the entry way to my flat in awe. I'm so excited to wake up every morning and be here. Buy fancy coffees on a Sunday morning, watch the street performers, laugh at the iPhone repairs guy that stands outside of the apple shop with a sign. I can't wait for it all.

I walk through the close and race myself up the stairs to get to my apartment door. Jimmying the door with my shoulder whilst I open the two locks. The door creaks as I open it.

It's perfect. *It's empty.* But it's perfect.

It's mainly all open floor. I've got the living room to my left which has a huge window that takes up most of the wall, to my right I have the kitchen with a big island. I've been in here a few times now when I was viewing it, but it looks so different now. It looks real now. I run around glancing at each area and double check all the taps and switches. My bedroom is full of natural light, the entirety on the wall is a window. (Slight exaggeration), I have a walk-through wardrobe which I plan to make a getting ready room and that leads to my bathroom. I'm so overwhelmed by it all. It is so surreal. I twirl around the living room admiring the view of the streets below me.

I'm on the third and top floor, there's only one apartment per floor. I keep saying 'apartment' because it makes it sound fancy, it's a flat.

Oh, now I need to unpack my car. Fuck my life.

Skipping down the stairs to my car, my little white fiat 500 looks tiny but it has eighteen years' worth of stuff in it. I wanted to do everything myself, I hate asking people for things, and in this newfound 'Ophelia' she is a lot more independent. I just don't want to need to rely on anyone anymore. Not on my mum, not on Blake. I just want to be myself. And become the best version of myself.

On the fourth trip up the stairs, I lose my mojo and start to slow down. *Why do I own so many books?* When I get to the bottom of the close, I see a set of familiar faces. Its Lacy and Dan.

"I knew that you would never ask for help so here we are." Dan says. Him and Lacy leaning against my car.

I smile, holding back tears. "You guys." I run up to them, wrapping my arms around them both. "Thank you." As much as I hate asking for help, I love receiving it. That's probably a lie, I'm a control freak. And a perfectionist.

"How did you get all this in here?" Dan huffs pulling out a box from under the driver's seat.

"Stop complaining. Let's get you moved in." Lacy tosses a pile of clothes over her shoulder, smiling at me.

I give them the official tour between trips up and down the stairs. Showing them the fancy shower that I don't know how to work yet and the cupboard that I will dedicate to cleaning supplies and the section of the living room that will be my office.

"Your car is empty." Dan sings, obviously very happy that he doesn't need to hoof boxes up a set of stairs anymore. I glance at the stack of boxes that have been dumped in the kitchen, then look back up at Dan, then over to Lacy.

"You are an idiot." She states, bending down to pick up a box. I chuckle. Dan puts his hands on him hips and sighs at the ceiling.

Once all the boxes are organised into each room Dan and Lacy lean against the wall in the living room. In the nicest way possible I want to tell them to fuck off. I appreciate them helping me move, but I want to spend the first night here myself. I don't have a bed, or a couch, or a pillow. All-nighter is it then. That actually sounds amazing, energy drinks and decorating and unpacking my apartment.

"Right. We better head. You're moving tomorrow." Lacy pats Dans head.

Dan is moving into student accommodation for university. His university is a ten-minute walk from here, so I'm sure he'll pop in unexpectedly to steal my snacks.

I give them away a half drank bottle of water for their help. I don't have any cups yet, so I'll be drinking out of the tap like a hamster until my packages arrive tomorrow.

Unpacking my life's belongings is suddenly so surreal. All of my life can be packed up into my tiny car. I thought that I had lived a pretty lived life. But apparently not. Reminiscing on all of my old pictures from my first day of primary school, my first lock of hair, concert tickets from bands I don't remember seeing or even liking that much, tiny nick naks that I've picked up on holidays. I feel so whole yet so empty, all of these things mean so much to me, yet I don't know why. I've held onto a tiny glass swan for, well as long as I remember, but I don't know where I got it. I'm sitting on the floor, on a pile of towels and a blanket, going through my belongings wondering. Wondering about Blake. Is he happy? Is he okay? Because I am. I don't think its spoken about enough of how after a serious or long-term relationship you come out of it a brand-new person and have a new perspective on life. I wonder is Blake has a new perspective on life yet. I hope he has found someone that can give him what he wants. Who has the same dreams and aspirations as him. Who can plan their future wedding with him and pick out kid's names. Those things that make people happy and warm inside make me want to be sick.

Me- Hi. I just wanted to see if you're, okay? X

I don't know if it's weird to text someone after breaking up with them almost three months ago. We haven't spoken since that night in my mum's kitchen. I want to make sure he's okay, because as much as I tell myself I don't, I still love him. And it's only natural to worry. According to my mum, he has a job in the barbers just down the street from my mum's work. I'm glad that I don't work there anymore, because I would absolutely 'accidentally' run into him to make sure he's okay. *He's taking longer to text back than he used to.* He might not want to speak to me though. I did break his heart. I saw how hurt he was that night, I hate how much I hurt him, the sadness in his eyes was undeniable, you'd think that the world was ending. I'm in denial about how much he means to me still. Even if I'm not 'in love' with him anymore he still helped me incredibly. And it's because of him that I am where I am. If I hadn't met Blake when I did, I know that I would not be living in Glasgow of all places, I wouldn't have launched a brand. I wouldn't be happy. Well, I'm trying to be happy anyway. I think I might be in denial about that too. These anti-depressants really do be kicking my ass most of the time.

Blake- Hi. I'm okay x

Me- Good, I'm always here for you. Thank you for everything you have done for me x

Blake- I just need time. Thank you for everything you have done for me too x

I'm glad he told me he's okay, even though he is most likely lying. But I never thought that he would say 'thank you for everything you have done for me too' I don't think I done anything spectacular for him. He done everything for me. He held me when I cried, nurtured me during panic attacks, took his time with me, he was gentle with me, he was there for me. All the time. And I broke up with him. I had no right to break up with him. He was amazing. His is amazing. I just couldn't let go of myself. I can't imagine living here with Blake. He told me before, he wants to have a house as a home, with three bedrooms, he wants a spectacular wedding and kids. He wanted a classic family. And I can't give him that. It breaks my heart that I can't give him that. He deserves it so much.

Mum- Happy moving night!! I'll let you get yourself settled. Let me know if I can help, next movie night is at yours. I am so proud of you. I love you. Xxx

I smile reading the text.

Me- Thank you mum. I think I want to do everything myself though. I'll let you know when everything is sorted. I love you too. Xxx

My mum knows me better than anyone, she knows that I want to do everything myself. I am a recluse, a hermit. I like my own company. I always have. And I also don't want someone helping me to be thrown back in my face. It sounds stupid, I know.

I stare out the window at the starry night, my apartment faces straight down onto a street, so I don't have another building blocking my view, I can see all the streetlights and people walking their dogs. I wonder what their stories are. Have they just moved out for the first time? Are they in Glasgow for work? I think I could sit here for days and watch people going about their business. Making up stories and profiles about them.

Its 2am. No sleep for me. I haven't eaten in twelve hours, which is a problem. Chinese food it is. It's weird saying a different address. I have never lived anywhere else before. I've always lived with my mum. I miss her. I've never slept in a house by myself before. Should I introduce myself to my neighbours? Is that a thing? Do I bake a cake for them? Not now. But I might bake them a cake. I will need to get things for cooking and baking first. I have approximately twenty-seven parcels coming tomorrow. My couch and my bed are being delivered between nine and two tomorrow. Why do delivery companies not give you a normal time window, say between nine and ten? Instead, I have to be here all day tomorrow wondering when my couch is being delivered. And I need to figure out how to use the washing machine. And the shower. And the oven. *Okay calm down Ophelia. you are eighteen. You have just moved into your first apartment by yourself. You do not need to know all these things yet. You do not need to bake your neighbours a cake. Your neighbours could be arseholes. You don't know them yet.*

Knock knock

Chinese food is here. Thank fuck I'm starving. "That's great, thank you so much." I say, handing over the delivery driver a crumpled £20 note and some coins I found in my bra for his trouble. I have never understood people who don't tip. Not their delivery drivers, taxi drivers, waiters, nail techs. Even if you just let them keep the change it might buy them their favourite drink, or a snack to have on their way home that will make their day a little bit better. I always make sure I leave a tip. Even when I go into my mum's salon, I always bring in cakes and drinks for everyone. I feel bad not paying for any of the treatments I get done so I go above and beyond any time I'm in. It's weird being in the salon and not working. Like anytime I'm in, I go over to the sterilisers and put tools in, if I notice a washing is needing done I do it. The girls always tell me off because it's not my job anymore, but it's engraved into me to do these things, I've been doing it since I was about ten.

I sit on top of the kitchen island with my legs crossed, my head close to banging off of the lampshade, with my chicken fried rice being spooned into my mouth with a prawn cracker. the stacks of books waiting for a bookshelf and all of my stock for Self-Care Co towering over the collection of fake plants.

"You did it Ophelia." I admire my space. "You did it." I didn't think that I would be in a financial place, a mental place or a career place to be able to live by myself. Starting my company was a huge risk, and it has *definitely* been worth it. moving here was risky, and I hope it's worth it. *I hope to fuck it's worth it.*

I finally got out of that small town. When you live in a small town with people who have always lived in a small town, you get taught to lower your expectations of your life. I never did. So that's why I left. The small town is what my mum wanted though. She is happy there. I wasn't. I used to want the small-town life, the farm fresh eggs from the corner shop, the constant waving and smiling at people that you've known all your life, as time went on, it made me sick. You would always be the same person and wouldn't have the opportunity to become a better version of yourself. I want to be a better version of myself.

Chapter 22

I have found the perfect little routine. I wake up at eight every morning, get dressed and have a cute walk down to my new favourite coffee shop, I go between a couple but my favourite one is my favourite because it plays spa music and the baristas wear funky pins on their aprons. I order a hazelnut latte and sometimes get a breakfast sandwich; I find a seat and work on my laptop for a couple of hours. Then head back up to my apartment to package orders and work. Then I'll usually head back down to the city centre and drop off my packaged orders at the post office. I've got to know the staff members at the post office, they hate me. To say the least. Basically, my workday is just a cute little day. One that I always wanted growing up. And the fact I get to call it work is incredible. My products get to sprinkle little bits of joy into other people's lives. That feeling is unmatched. When I'm not lugging boxes of stock up the stairs anyways. The delivery driver used to bring the boxes up for me but now I help him, going up three flights of stairs multiple times isn't in his job description. It probably is, but it shouldn't be.

This morning on my walk down to my favourite coffee shop its cold, but the sun is out, bouncing across the buildings, blinding my eyes. Ordering my coffee and egg and bacon sandwich as usual, grabbing a handful of sugar packets from the bench, and getting my usual seat in the back corner where the lights are low, and so I can watch everyone order their coffee and guess their jobs. My laptop is full of battery, and I am ready to go, but I can't, I can feel eyes on me. I look up momentarily from my laptop. I see him, a picture of perfection. The cheeky smile looks into my soul from across the coffee shop. I've never seen him here before; I've been to this coffee shop at least twice a week since I moved. He is a ray of sunshine, the golden glow surrounds him, his almost sparkly hair swoops across his face effortlessly, his round glasses catch the light at just the right angle to alight his brown, green eyes. And he's looking at me. His eyes inspect me from across the room. He has a laptop with him too, I wonder if he's working. Maybe he's working on a secret project that he hasn't told anyone about yet, I feel a light switch on in my soul. He flashes his pearlescent teeth. He is wearing a clean yet worn white t-shirt. My lips press themselves against each other before smiling back at him. I haven't smiled at someone flirtily since Blake. I haven't imagined myself moving on from Blake yet. Even though I know that he has moved on from me. Which as sad as it makes me feel, I am happy for him. Mystery man, looks me up and down, rubbing his hand across his face. Biting my lip making eyes that say, 'you're cute stranger'. I think my eyes worked because he swaggers over with confidence. But not cockiness. There's a big difference. He holds his laptop in one hand and his coffee in the other. I lean forward in my chair, putting my face in my hands to disguise my giddiness.

"Hello. My name is Cole. Can I sit here?" He asks. His statement less up front than I thought I would be considering how he swaggers when he walks.

"Hi Cole. My names Ophelia. Yes, you can sit there." I giggle when I say it because it sounds so ridiculous. Not the part where someone asks to sit with me, but the situation of my life. Straight from a movie. One of the movies where I skip half of it because it makes me feel sick. He pulls out the chair and starts typing away on his laptop. Almost ignoring the fact that I'm here. "Do you usually sit with strangers in coffee shops Cole?" My laptop screen has gone black because I haven't wiggled my mouse in since he's sat down. I stare at him looking down at his laptop.

"Only the pretty ones." He smirks, looking away from the screen at me. Then he goes back to the screen. I go back to my screen too. Too distracted now to reply to emails. So, I fiddle around with my mouse and end up writing…

Dear diary,

As I'm writing this there's a gorgeous man sitting in front of me. I think he is focusing on whatever he is doing on his laptop, but I can't distract myself from him. Should I feel guilty? About wanting to move on from Blake? Should I ask him to move back to his original seat? No because I like the fact that he is sitting across from me. I like the fact that he had the confidence to approach me. And I like the fact that I didn't get up and leave when he smiled at me. Someone who isn't ready to move on wouldn't still be sitting here. His name is Cole. He is wearing a silver ring on his pinkie, and he is drinking what looks like a latte, I can smell the cinnamon on the top of the mug. I like cinnamon. Almost as much as I like my hazelnut latte. Which is almost finished, and I want to go up and order another one, but I don't want to leave this table. So, I'm just going to keep pretending that I'm working.

Speaking of working I'm launching my new products next week. I have got notebooks, notepads and bookmarks made. I will most definitely be keeping a bundle for myself since I am obsessed with stationary. Oh, and I finally finished decorating my apartment a month later. I've successfully divided my living room, using a huge desk that I pack all my orders on, I've got a massive set of shelves that I store all of my stock on. I've moved my couch to the other side of the desk so I can't see my workspace when I'm on the couch. And I hung a projector up instead of a tv and I can link it up to my laptop. And it gets me out of paying a television license. There's bright, funky decorations everywhere, even in the bathroom. I've got neon sign that says... 'please don't do coke in the bathroom'. It's my prized possession. And not just because I spent way too much money on it. I had it in my head that it would be a talking point if I had parties, then I realised that I have approximately two friends. Well, three. I don't know if you'd consider your ex that you haven't spoken to properly since you broke up your friend. I hope we can still be friends.

Anyway, this man, Cole sitting in front of me, still hasn't started a conversation.

Love Lia

Xox

"I'm trying to act really cool about this by the way, but this has never happened to me." I blurt out, finishing the dregs of my coffee. I lift my head from my laptop.

"I've never done this before either and I was hoping you had." The confidence in his voice mellows and more of his personality becomes present. He seems goofy, sarcastic and nervous.

"I think this is the part where you're supposed to order me another coffee." I laugh, tapping my finger to the rim of my mug. He glugs the last mouthful of his coffee. Dragging his eyes between me and my mug. "Hazelnut with coconut milk." He flashes a thumbs up. Almost tripping as he gets out of the chair.

What the actual fuck. A man that I just met, is getting me coffee. Okay. Okay. *Well, that's happening.*

After a few minutes, he comes back over with the tray of our coffees and a few cakes. "I was not sure what cakes you liked so I got a few." I grin at him as he carefully placed the tray between our laptops. I close mine over and put it in my bag. "Oh crap." He says it like a cartoon. Running over to the table he was originally sat at, retrieving his backpack. I giggle as he prances back. He reminds me of the guys that bullied me in school. But he is nice. I think he is anyway. He cuts up the cakes in half, a white chocolate and raspberry muffin, empire biscuit and a cherry Bakewell. "Do you want the cherry off of the Bakewell?" He asks, carefully places the halves of the other cakes onto individual plates.

"I'm actually allergic to cherries." I see him panic.

"Oh well, we'll just keep that far away from you then." He keeps the cherry on the original plate and slides the plate away from me.

"Thank you." I stir some sugar into my coffee. "So, what brings you here?" I curiously ask, tapping the spoon on the side of the mug.

"If you mean in Glasgow, I've lived here since university. But if you mean over to this table, I promised myself that I would put myself out there more." Shaking a brown sugar packet. "Dare I ask you?"

"I just moved here a month ago, but I've lived thirty minutes away all my life. I promised myself I would keep to myself, so you are lucky that I am still sitting here." I want so badly to not care about anyone but myself, but I can't help but feel interested and care for other people. No matter how hard I try not to. "What do you do?" I pull apart a piece of the muffin.

"I'm an editor for Read Well Publishing." He takes the other half of the white chocolate muffin. "It's more exciting than it sounds." He says defensively before shoving the muffin in his mouth. He wipes his hands with a napkin between mouthfuls. For the first time in a long time. I don't feel nervous, on edge, scared, I feel at ease, comfortable, happy sitting here speaking to a stranger. But something tells me that he won't be a stranger for very much longer.

I feel glittery inside and I can't help but assume that my face is showing it. Blushing every time, he looks at me. "I'm trying not to speak too much because I tend to ramble and waffle on."

"I want to hear your voice." He whispers. Taking the final piece of his half of the muffin.

"Okay. Five quick fire facts about me. One, I have a fascination with the titanic. Two, my favourite tv show is friends, three, my favourite friend's character is Phoebe. Four, my favourite colour is pink even though when I was younger, I told everyone it was blue to seem different and quirky. And five, my love language is words of affection." Okay I didn't even know those things about myself.

"That is quite a list Ophelia. Okay my turn, quickly because my boss is going to kill me if I show up to work late." He checks his watch. "One, my favourite tv show is also friends, two my favourite friend's character is Chandler. Three, I would love to take you out for dinner some time, four, I think you're really beautiful and five, my love language is physical touch." He blushes when he says his facts.

"I think you just wasted two of your facts." I trail my tongue across the backs of my teeth. "I would love to go out for dinner." I admit. I don't want to admit it though. My tough exterior is breaking down. And melting together with his very soft, cheeky interior that for some reason I feel comfortable melting in front of.

"Okay good." He shakes the nerves off of him. He passes me his phone and I put my number in it.

"I'm free on Saturday." I say, texting myself from his phone so I can save his number. I feel giddy as he stands up to leave. I stand up too. He's not much taller than me, maybe an inch or two, enough to make me feel safe. "It was nice meeting you Cole." I go back and forth with giving him a hug. He can see it on my face, he opens his arms inviting me in.

"It was nice meeting you too Ophelia." We have a non-awkward side hug. He smells sweet. Like we might use the same shower gel, his clothes smell fresh as well, he places his hand on my shoulder and gently pulls me in. "I'll text you." He waves back at me when he leaves the coffee shop, I don't stop looking at him while he zig zags his way through crowd of tables.

The walk back up to my apartment was more of a skip. But I'm also scared. Did I really just agree to go on a date with someone? I need advice on this. No Lia, you need to be a big girl. Do what you want, when you want, as long as you're not hurting anyone. But am I hurting someone? What about Blake? Blake has been dating someone. It's quick, and way too soon, but he is. Dan seen it on Instagram. They've been dating for two weeks but have already made it official. Blake has finally found someone that can fall as hard as him. But does that mean it's okay for me to date? Fuck knows.

Jumping into my apartment, picking up my post on the way in.

Ping

My phone vibrates in my pocket.

Cole- Hi. I've booked a table at TGIs for Saturday at 4.

He doesn't send kisses when he texts. That is off putting.

Me- Hi, great, I'll meet you there xx

Cole- Great. I'm looking forward to it. xx

There we go. That's more like it. It's important to me that kisses get sent to me after a text. It means a lot. I have four days to prepare. *Fuck.*

"Lacy. If I told you that I had a potential first date today, what would you tell me to wear?" I leap over the pile of clothes in my wardrobe, holding my phone to my ear.

"Get your boobs out gal!" She shouts.

Holding my hands on my hips, disappointed at her unsophisticated answer. "Lacy!" I shout.

"Sorry." She laughs. "Wear something comfortable yet impressive." I can imagine her pointing her finger over the phone.

"So, about zero percent of my clothes. Great"

I settle on my leather look trousers that squeak when I walk and my pink scoop neck top, that with the right bra, pushes the girls up nicely without flashing someone. In the process of getting dressed I flash the whole of Glasgow. I still haven't found curtains long or wide enough to cover my windows. It's not like that many people are going to be looking three stories up.

Cole- I'm just leaving my flat, let me know when you're here. xx

Shit. Its 3.40. and TGI Fridays is a fifteen-minute walk, and I haven't done my makeup yet. *Fuck.*

Me- Leaving in 5. X

I definitely will not be leaving for another ten minutes. Slapping on bronzer and puckering up my lips, flipping my freshly curled hair to loosen the tight curls. Chucking my purse, lip gloss and phone into my bag that I got off of the back of my door. Slamming my door shut before I jiggle the keys to lock it. Rushing down the close.

Making the sprint to Buchanan Street. 3.52pm. Nearly running into the fake beggar as I turn the corner. I can see TGIs in the distance, slowing down my speed walk so that I'm not out of breath by the time I go inside. I feel like I know these streets like the back of my hand by now. Even though I only moved a month ago, I was here every few months as a kid. I used to hate it, hate how busy it was. Now I'm down in the centre every chance I get, I'm looking forward to the Christmas lights coming on and the Christmas markets, with the German hotdogs and the nut and sweet stalls. All ridiculously overpriced but it's worth it. I used to go to the Christmas markets every year when I was young, I haven't been in a few years.

Me- I'm here. x

I text him as I walk in, when I look up, he is waving at me from across the restaurant. *Here we go.*

Chapter 23

"You look amazing." Cole stands up from his seat, pulling mine out for me real gentleman like.

"Thank you. So do you." I glance at his attire before I sit down. He is wearing a black ribbed t-shirt with black trousers. I go nervous for a minute. His hand hovers over my lower back as I sit.

He pushes his glasses up the bridge of his nose. Eyeing up the cocktail menu. I pretend to read it. I didn't realise how awkward first dates were. Since I've never really had one before. "This is my first proper first date by the way so I'm going to need you to take the lead on this." I look up from the menu biting my lip.

"Well, I think it's supposed to be a lot of awkward silences and feet touching under the table." He jolts his feet to mine. And laughs. "Tell me everything about yourself Ophelia."

"Well, I'm eighteen, almost nineteen."

"You're eighteen?" He almost chokes on his water. I nod. "You could have fooled me for at least twenty-two, you're so mature."

"I'm going to take that as a compliment Cole and going to guess that you are at least twenty." I sip on my water.

"Twenty-three actually." Correcting me. "How in the hell, did you end up moving out to Glasgow so young?" He seems genuinely impressed with me. Which is something I like. I enjoy talking about myself, as sociopathic as that sounds.

Our conversation pauses as the waitress takes our orders. I order a long island iced tea for my drink and a sirloin steak with the special sauce, Cole orders a purple rain and legendary glaze burger. I don't think of it when I order, but there are so many women that would be put off ordering a steak to not emasculate their date. I'm just past that point in my life now.

"I own my own business. I design apparel and very soon stationary." It's still weird saying that that is my job. It was so much easier saying that I was a beauty therapist, because no one ever asked any follow up questions. They just thought I gave facials all day.

"Okay. That's impressive. How did you get into that?" I love the fact that he's asking me so many questions, I've went my whole life asking other people questions about their life and it's a nice change of pace being asked questions for a change.

"That's enough about me. How did you get into publishing?" I start cutting up my steak.

"Well. I've read my whole life and it just made sense, I went through university and have worked my way up to be an editor. I mainly edit romance which doesn't make much sense, but it seems to do well." A romance editor strangely makes a lot of sense about him. He's really gentle and funny and sweet. I haven't once thought about Blake tonight. I don't want to think about Blake when I'm around Cole. Watching him squash his burger into his mouth isn't disgusting or weird. It's perfect. Cole is a breath of fresh air. Cole doesn't know anything about what happened to me. I'm not a delicate house of cards that is about to blow over. I'm not defined by my past, not defined by my mum or my dad or by shit friends. I'm just me. I think I like being myself. For once.

I wave over to the waitress for the bill, doing the universal hand movement. You know what I mean. Cole gets his wallet out, his hand on the bill before it hits the table. "Don't you dare sneaky." I grab it off of him before he has the chance to see how much it costs.

"Emm, excuse me. I think it's part of first date etiquette for the man to pay." He tries to slide his hand around me to get it off of me.

"Well, you obviously haven't had a first date with me before." I put my card down on the receipt.

"Split?"

"If it would recover some of your masculinity then fine." I smile, pushing my tongue to the inside of my lip. His card meets mine on the receipt. His eyes stare deep into mine and all I can think of is how I really want to kiss him, banging my feet against his under the table. "Do you want to come back to my apartment for a drink?" My breath trembles as I ask. I didn't think twice about that. Cole is a nice guy. A guy that I feel comfortable being in my flat. Unsure of his answer because of his lack of enthusiasm in his breathing.

His brownish, greenish eyes trace along my face. "I'd love too." He whispers, saying it so perfectly. Okay this is the first time someone is coming to my apartment other than Lacy, Dan or my mum. High stakes here.

Latching each other's arms as we leave our table. He makes sure to jump in front of me and opens the door. "Thank you." I say waiting for him at the other side of the door. Our arms are latched again. I wish I brought a jacket. It's September which means that it's too cold to be considered summer and too warm to be considered autumn. "I used to hate Glasgow." I hate silence.

"Why?" He says defensively.

"I grew up in a tiny town and Glasgow was intimidating and busy and there were so many different kinds of people." I tighten my grip on his arm, leaning my head on his shoulder for warmth.

"I grew up about ten minutes away on the train. I came to school here, university here, work here. My dad got a good job about a few hours away, so my family moved when I was in my last year of university." He has a happy family. "My dad works in accounting. It's really boring and my mum is a teacher for children with assisted needs, but she does it part time now." His life seems perfect. "What about you?"

I don't want to answer him so I dilly dally in constructing my answer. "Uh. My mum is a beauty therapist. She has her own salon and training academy. My dad." I can't remember what my dad does. It's been over a year since I've text him. That's ridiculous. I don't know what my dads' jobs is. "I think my dad works in construction." The words fall out of my mouth. Cole doesn't react to the last part of my answer. I think he can sense that it's weird for me to talk about. The streetlights ping on as we turn the corner. "Do you have any siblings?" I hate talking about families, why did I ask him?

"Yes. I've got an older brother at twenty-seven and a little sister at sixteen." The perfect family.

"I'm an only child." I was also an accident, but I feel like I shouldn't say that. I can imagine Cole's childhood. Proper and amazing. A full house all of the time. He was never alone. His siblings and him must be so close. His mum and dad are happily married and living their life properly before they retire early and have three weeklong tropical holidays and fritter away half of their savings. I picture him having a cleaner. In his house growing up. Not a full time cleaner, but a once a week, hoover the stairs, change the bedsheets cleaner who does origami on the toilet rolls. I juggle the keys on my way up the close. Passing my neighbours doors. I still haven't baked them a cake, or introduced myself, I haven't seen them to be fair, I haven't heard them either other than hearing them shout at the tv watching football. I think it's an older couple that lives on the first floor, because outside their door is a welcome door mat and a cute table with a flowerpot on it, something I only imagine an older couple having.

I swing my door open for Cole, struggling to jiggle the keys out of the lock. Kicking my shoes off and putting them on my shoe rack at the door. Throwing my keys on top of the shoe shelf in my key bowl next to my car keys. There was no point in me buying a car. I drive it once a week, twice tops, when I get all my food shopping done. I walk everywhere or take the train if I want to be fancy. Going straight to the kitchen to wash my hands. I've gotten into the habit of washing my hands every time I've been out. I would usually take my makeup off if I'm in for the night, but since I have company that part if my routine will have to wait.

"Your apartment is stunning." Cole glances around the room, circling the area. "Can use your bathroom?"

"Of course." I point him towards it. He tip-toes his way through. "Okay Ophelia, there is a man in your apartment. A very nice man. Who seems like a good man. And he is in your bathroom." I say to myself quietly whilst getting a bottle of wine out of the freezer. Someone bought me this bottle when I moved in, I think it was one of my old clients from the salon. I hate wine, but I can't stand it taking up room anymore. Grabbing glasses from the cupboard.

"Okay that sign in the bathroom is incredible." He laughs. "I did not do coke in your bathroom by the way."

We make our way over to the couch, I load up my laptop with an episode of friends to go on the projector, bringing the glasses and the bottle of wine with me. Cole sits on the other end of the couch; my knees are up at my chest and the wine is in my mouth. Relaxing on my couch, sipping on my second glass of wine. Cole is splayed out on the other side of the couch, laughing at my bad jokes about friends. I like the fact that he's laughing, he has such a hearty laugh, like a proper chuckle that is contagious. His hand is behind my neck on the back of the couch, and I can't stop thinking. Thinking about how I'm not ready for this. My past keeps haunting me. Thinking about how much I want to be loved yet being loved means giving up a part of myself and I don't want to lose myself again. I can't lose myself again.

"Okay, Cole. Before this goes any further. I need to tell you something." I sip the last dregs of my glass. "I just got out of a serious relationship." I pause. "I can't get into anything serious right now." I regret the words. Why do I let my mind control my future? Why does my past need to have anything to do with my future?

Cole pours himself another glass. "Why did your last relationship end?" He queries. I don't know how to answer without making myself out to be an arsehole.

"He loved me more than I loved him." I refill my glass, snatching the bottle from Cole, tipping the dregs into my glass. "I regret ending it like I did." I admit. I haven't spoken about my breakup with Blake with anyone. Not even mum or Dan or Lacy.

"How did you end it?" He sips. Sensing the tension in my throat. "You don't need to answer me I'm just curious."

"No, its fine. It's just hard to speak about. We were together for just under a year and a half. I had a lot of issues. Have a lot of issues." I correct myself. "He wanted a future, and I couldn't promise him one." I bite at the inside of my lip, staring into the wine glass. "He helped me overcome a lot of things. I'm ready to move on from him. I just can't rush into anything." I apologise without apologising.

"Well. We can keep this chill. No need to rush into anything. I know this is our first date and all, but I do like you and I don't mind keeping this casual. And I'm not the kind of man that dates multiple women at once."

"Thank you." Whispering my words because my heart is screaming at me to kiss him. Another glass of cheap wine later and I can feel our two bodies being pulled together. I can't kiss him. I can't cheapen a first kiss with someone over a glass of wine too many. "Do you believe in love Cole?" My voice turns serious and harsh. I don't want it to be serious and harsh.

He pauses for a moment, fighting his answer. "The easiest answer is yes. But I don't think that love can be defined in such simple words. Love is so much more than a black or white answer like yes or no. Love is complex. Love isn't a thing that a flip switch and it's there. Love is an hourglass, love slowly trickles its way into your life so subtly that you don't notice it. And if you go too long without noticing it. Time runs out." You can tell that he works with romance novels. "I read and edit romance novels all day and I have read thousands of analogies and metaphors for what you would describe love as, but nothing can define it." I can feel tears well up in my eyes with how beautiful his words are. I want him to kiss me. He checks his watch. "I'm going to head home. Thank you so much for tonight." He stands up before I get the chance to react. His words are so defined and pronounced so perfectly and romantically but he doesn't know how to act when he says these things. It's frustrating. But it sums him up so perfectly. Grabbing his coat from the side of the island.

"I've had a really good time tonight." Croaking my words with a lump in my throat. He heads to the door. I place the wine glass that I've been cradling for the past hour on the work top.

Before he reaches for the handle, he turns round to face me standing up from the couch. "So have I." His eyes look me up and down as I approach him. Feeling both our breaths tremble as I edge closer to him, he slowly leans into me, I go slightly onto my tip toes, our lips barley touching and it feels like fireworks, feeling each other breathing. Our lips collide so intensely that I grip onto his shoulders, breathing into his mouth as the kiss stops. My hands relaxed around the back of his neck. Our eyes meet again, not for long because our lips are together again,

Coles hands are around my waist and in my hair and everywhere I want them to be. I've never felt a first kiss like this. I'm not scared, I'm not wondering if I'm being watched. I'm just enjoying this kiss. Enjoying every time his tongue slides across mine, every time our teeth clash against each other's, but we don't care because we're enjoying it too much. Gasping for air anytime his hand moves through my hair. We part. I press my top and bottom lips against one another to savour the taste. "Good night, Ophelia. I'll text you." He whispers, grazing his thumb across my cheek, still holding my face in his hand. I am left speechless. In a good way. He reaches for the door and quietly closes it on his way out. I watch him leave through my peephole, pressing myself against the door. Once he is out of my eyesight I lean my back against the door, slowly falling down onto the floor. Out of words at how amazing that kiss was. I want to kiss him again. I can hear his steps echo the stairs. Oh god I want to kiss him again. I really want to kiss him again. *Oh fuck I want to kiss him again.*

Chapter 24

Dear diary,

I had a first date last tonight, my first date since Blake. I met him at the coffee shop on Thursday. He is funny and nervous and everything Blake wasn't. Well, he is a good kisser like Blake. If we went to school together, we would definitely have dated. He is a few years older than me which I think is why I enjoyed his company. He doesn't know anything about me. My past anyway. I like that. I felt like Blake defined me by my trauma and not by who I am. I hated that. Is it weird that I kind of liked the fact that Cole was nervous? For once I was the confident one in the situation. I think Cole liked that. Cole has a beautiful energy, like the kind of guy that would make the perfect pet. That sounds bad. Like he is just joyful and wants to be near you, but also gives you space. We had our first date and first kiss and he hasn't text me. Some women would say that that makes them panic, that they must hate them, don't want to see them again. I would feel caged and suffocated if Cole text me right now. Don't get me wrong I would love to text him right now and set up another date, but I want to make that decision, the toxic part of me wants to make him wait and be extra excited when he sees me next. On the other hand, the hopelessly romantic side of me wants to phone him right now and tell him to kiss me again and that I want to spend all day kissing him and going on another date. But that's not very girl boss of me. Why do I need to choose what part of me I get to show to people? I don't want to be a cold-hearted bitch and I

don't want to be a dopey wide-eyed teenager. How do I
find a happy medium?

Love Lia

xox

Okay it's been fourteen hours since I kissed Cole. I got up, had my morning walk and my cleaning ritual Sunday morning. That's one thing I do that's the same as my mum's house. I spot clean everyday but on Sundays all hell breaks loose, the couch gets pulled out, bedsheets get washed, bleached floors. I was a bit fragile this morning after my bottle of wine and cocktail from last night. I think it's been an appropriate amount of time to text Cole. Flinging myself onto my freshly hoovered couch, kicking my feet in the air when I grab my phone from the table, considering whether or not to invite Cole back over.

Me- Hi, I had a great time last night. Xx

That sounds normal, right?

Cole- Hi, I really enjoyed it, do you fancy going out tonight as well? Don't worry if you don't. xx

Me- Of course! Xx

That sounded way too enthusiastic and desperate.

Cole- Great, I'll pick you up in about an hour? Xx

Me- See you soon. Xx

An hour? Considering the fact that I stink of bleach and haven't gotten out of the clothes that I slept in last night,

I'm asking a lot of myself. Sighing as I look around my apartment, the space is so clean and tidy, immaculate almost, I am the complete opposite, I don't even think I put deodorant on this morning. Shower time for me. I don't have time for a proper 'the shower', I usually spend my Sunday nights doing that, now I'm going out? On a Sunday? That's not like me. Who is this woman? What does a second date entail? What are the expectations of a second date? Where are we going? Drying my body off half hazardly, slipping on the bathmat as I sprint to find clothes to wear. Forty-four minutes, time is ticking.

"Okay Lia. What says, want to make out? but also says, I am a lady with zero issues?" Saying to myself, studying my wardrobe rails, flipping the items around to get a better look. "This works." I shrug, dropping my towel and pulling the lace body suit over myself, scooping my boobs in. When I moved I basically redone my entire wardrobe, I definitely hadn't been taking my medication at the time because I had packed it away in a box, but I went out one afternoon and spent a small fortune on new risky clothes, this body suit being one of them, like you could absolutely wear it in the bedroom, but pair it with a black blazer and you're ready for a day at the office at a multi-billion pound tech company. I'm going for the tech company look tonight.

Slicking my hair back into a low ponytail because tonight is supposed to be hair wash night and my hair is absolutely disgustingly greasy, dancing to my hype music, I need to be hyped up tonight, because if I'm being honest with myself, I'm extremely nervous. Cole is such a good guy. Then I'm here. Even though, I'm not a silly teenager who lives with her mum and works in her salon, I still feel like I am. I think everything just happened to fast; my mind hasn't had time to adapt to the new me. Cole works for a publishing company, that's a big boy job, like suit and tie big boy job. I go to work in joggers and a hoodie with unwashed hair. So, I feel like I need to make a good impression to him that I'm not a slob. I'm definitely not a slob, I just prefer comfort, I'm remembering that I enjoy comfort as I'm leaning over my toilet trying to re button the poppers on the gusset of this body suit. Twenty minutes. Puffing my cheeks whilst I blend in my concealer, getting mascara under my eyes and completely ruining my concealer. Great.

Knock knock

 He's early.

Running through the apartment to unlock the door.

"Hi Cole." I smile opening the door, pretending that my bathroom doesn't have makeup all over the worktops.

"Hi Ophelia." He holds his arms out to me. I fall into them, smelling his aftershave on his neck. "You look amazing." He grins.

"I'll be five minutes, make yourself comfortable." I rush back off into the bathroom, still sliding on the floor with my slippers. I didn't even take the time to notice him and appreciate his presence. He's wearing dark trousers, with boots and a fancy t shirt, tucked in, and a black coat. I think that outfit makes sense next to mines. He has just shaved his face, because it felt smoother than last night, his skin felt cold, so that's why he's wearing a coat. Slipping on my blazer and my jazzy boots, shoving a few necklaces on to create the illusion that I'm a put together person.

When I come back into the living room, he's sitting upright on the couch, not relaxed at all, looking around at my nick naks on the shelves and walls. "Everything looks so clean; I didn't want to ruin it." He stands back up, smoothing out the couch with his hand.

I giggle. That's such a me thing to do. "I um. I'm glad that you wanted to go out again tonight." That was a half lie. Of course, I wanted to see him again, but I also really wanted to wash my hair and shave my legs. *Shit, should I have shaved my legs? Is that second date etiquette?*

"Well, last night, was the first time I had went out on a date for about a year. So, I have a few dates to make up for." He admits as I grab my bag from the back of the door.

"How come?" I ask. "You don't need to answer me." I snap back. My toxic trait is being too nosey and asking too many personal questions."

"Don't be silly. My ex-girlfriend was an arsehole."

"Amen." Checking my bag to make sure I have everything. Keys, in my hand, purse, check, phone, check, lip gloss, check. Ready to go. "Well last night was my first date in a long time." I would never say that me and Blake dated. We went out to eat a few times, but we mainly sat in his car or in my mum's house, and I liked that, I didn't want to go out and try new restaurants or to see new places. I want to do that now though. Cole stands beside me as I lock the door. Holding his arm in a loop for me. "I didn't tell you, but you look really nice." I say as we take our time going down the steps. "I should've told you when I saw you."

"Thank you." He grips his arm, tighter to his body, pulling me closer to him. We get to the end of the close and onto the street.

"So, what are we doing?" I ask, turning my body to him.

"Well. I thought we could just walk around until we find somewhere to go into. Then maybe kiss like we did last night." He smirks. I hold my tongue between my teeth, biting my lip. Feeling butterflies, reminiscing on our amazing kiss from last night. It was amazing, so powerful and yet soft and yet still intense. Our connection was impeccable. Its scary to say that though. I'll assume that Cole feels the same way, or he wouldn't ask me out again tonight. I'll imagine that anyway.

"I think that sounds really nice." My voice goes quite and nervous. But I'm not nervous. I'm doing everything in my power to not say 'can we please just about turn and kiss on my couch and then end up naked please.' But I'm dressed like a lady tonight, lady in the streets and freak in the sheets is what I like to think. Vanilla is the new kinky apparently. Stopping to button up my blazer, Coles arms still looped around mine. The Glasgow sky turns pink as the sun begins to set, that's one of the things I miss about living in a small town. There was always a good spot to watch the sunset. Always an empty field to sit in and watch the twinkly stars come out. It's rare for me to see the sunset now because of all the buildings and telegraph poles in the way of the sky. The streets are mostly empty except from the shoppers stumbling out of Primark. "Do you fancy just getting the chippy?" I ask, smelling the stench of chip fat from under central station.

"I am so glad you said that, because that is exactly what I want right now." Cole sighs with joy. "And then we can find a bench and quiz each other on ourselves."

Cole insists on paying for our fish suppers. Throwing the newspaper wrapping in the bin as we find a bench. We each sit cross legged across from each other, the smell of vinegar soaking our hands.

"Okay, if you could change one thing about yourself, what would it be?" I ask, stabbing at my chips with the wooden fork. I love asking people deep questions about themselves. Some would say that it's a toxic trait

"Good question. I've always dislike how nervous I can be. But then in the same breath be confident. I've always been like that; I don't understand it." He picks apart his fish that's smothered in brown sauce.

"I get what you mean, like one minute you're being talkative and direct with your words then the next you go quiet and timid."

He nods. "Your turn."

"I don't do it so much now. But I used to lie when people asked how I was. I would always say that I was fine when I wasn't. It really annoyed me; I've been trying to get out of that habit lately." I say, blowing on a chip. I think that I'm getting a lot better at it. And if I catch myself doing it, I correct myself. I don't know why I always ignored my emotions and didn't let anyone know how I was feeling.

"I do that sometimes too. I think that its scary to admit how much things get to you, especially if they're little things, then you're scared that the other person will be annoyed for you being annoyed at something they're doing that annoys you. That was way too many words that came out of my mouth there. Apologies." He laughs.

I laugh too. "I um." I pause before I continue. "I had some stuff happen in my life. For a while I pretended, I was okay."

"Are you okay now?" He asks sincerely.

"I am. I really am." I smile down at my legs once I've said it. Cole's hand grips my knee comforting me. I really am doing good. The streetlights clink on, illuminating us on the bench. My legs start cramping up from being crossed for too long. I'm not seven anymore sitting with my legs in a basket in front of the black board at school. Oh, memories. I uncross my legs so there's one leg on either side of the bench. We're mostly silent, the crinkling of papers and the sound of the crispy chips landing on the ground when the fork snaps them in half and send them flying. I leave a few chips in the wrapper. "Do you want the last of these chips?" I angle the tray to Cole.

"Thank you." He squeals like a child, stacking the few chips onto his fork, leaning his head back and biting them off the fork. I like how funny and goofy he is. I don't even think he means it. I notice how he dances when he's eating food he really likes, he gives his shoulders a little wiggle. And he pushes his glasses up his face using his pinkie. "Do you ever wonder why the world brings two people together?" I shake my head smiling at his question. Never date someone who reads romance novels for a living because they are going to throw some deep ass questions at you.

"Well. I think that the universe works in mysterious ways. like when I met you yesterday in the coffee shop, I hadn't been in that coffee shop in weeks. And I usually start work at nine, but it just so happens that yesterday there was a later start and I thought to myself, 'I'll just go grab a coffee at that place a used to go to.' I think that everything happens for a reason, no matter how much it hurts you, no matter how much you don't want it to happen, it happens because then something else will happen, and something else, and something else."

I hate that logic. But I also love it. Brian raped me. Which hurt me. Then Blake came into my life. Then I started a company. Then I broke up with Blake. I ended up alone again. I moved to a different city. And now I'm happy. But I was also happy before Brian raped me. Life is a full circle and sometimes things happen and sometimes things that you want to happen don't happen. It feels morbid to say 'I'm glad Brian raped me' which I'm obviously not, but I'm glad for what happened afterwards. I met Blake. Which I probably wouldn't have even become friend with him because he was so intimidating to me, but I had been through the worst, so I had nothing to lose. And Blake quite literally fixed me. He showed me how a man is supposed to treat a woman. Which is old fashioned of me, but I don't think there's anything nicer than a man holding a door open for you, or holding your hand, or telling you that you're beautiful. They're all very basic things for me that I check off my list because of Blake. Blake made me realise that I had more to offer, that I had to get out of the same routines, the same people. Blake fixed me until I broke again. Blake taught me that I could be fixed. I just had to fix myself this time. I hope I don't break again.

Chapter 25

Cole scrunches up the wrappers and tosses them into the bin next to us. The sky is dark now. It's getting late. "Do you want to go back to mines?" I timidly ask. Again, because I'm trying to stop myself from saying 'do you want to kiss until we're naked?' Because that's exactly what I want to say and do.

"Absolutely." He reaches out for my hand, his hands are cold, I lean my head on his shoulder before we start the climb up to my apartment. He kisses my forehead. His lips are warm. I adjust myself in this body suit, the poppers undone themselves as soon as I sat on the bench, I'm hoping that they've not wriggled up to look like I've got a nappy on. *But to be honest I couldn't give a fuck.* I like how touchy Cole is, always has a hand on me, it's a subtle thing that most people wouldn't think about, but I notice it.

The streetlights brighten the pavements, all of the restaurant's rubbish sits out beside their doors, cluttering the streets. That's one thing about Glasgow I don't like, the mess. There is always rubbish lying, constantly bin lorries driving around stinking up the streets. But it's a small price to pay for a beautiful city.

Holding the main door open for me as we stoat into my building. His hand on the small of my back as we clumber up the stairs. Giggling like giddy teenagers because I think we both know what we each desire right now. Dropping my keys twice before we reach the top of the stairs.

The door is slammed shut and Cole is up against it, grabbing my waist, I drop my bag at the side of me, my mouth is on his, my hands on his neck and his shoulders and his face. I'm still kissing him throwing off my blazer and kicking off my shoes, Cole does the same, our jackets in a pile on the floor, I back up leading him to my bedroom, our lips still locked together. Our kissing is intense, I press myself into him on my bedsheets, feeling him back away slightly. "Are you okay?" I ask, whispering.

"Yeah, is this, okay? Do you want to have sex?" He asks.

"Yes, I want to have sex with you Cole." I laugh, I thought I was being full on, putting myself out there and being clear that I wanted to have sex. But apparently not, or he is just being sure. I think I like that. "Do you want to have sex with me?"

"Absolutely." Grabbing my face back in with his hand, flipping me over so I'm underneath him. I laugh, raking my hands though his hair as his lips cover my collar bone, working their way back up to my neck then to my face. I don't want to be anywhere else right now. I want to be right here. Me and Cole have a connection, a connection that is undeniable, we are alike and completely different at the same time. Our souls are the same. We have had different up bringing but somehow by some miracle we've came together. "Your skin tastes so nice." He exclaims. His tongue sliding down my jaw. His hands trying to figure out how to get this top off me, I pull the undone poppers of the bodysuit up over my trousers. I sit up while Cole helps me rip off my top, whilst ripping his off too. His hand gliding up the back of my thigh as I warp my leg around his hips.

"I really like you, Cole." I say dragging my hand across his shoulders. "And that really scares me." Saying it releases all the tension that my body has been holding for the past eighteen years. I didn't lie. I'm not crying but I can tell by the look on Cole's face that he knows that it was hard for me to say.

"It scares me too. But we can be scared together." He tucks my hair behind my ear, gently leaning down and kissing my lips softly, biting his lip when he pulls away. I want to be scared with Cole. My bed becomes a swimming pool and our movements become liquid. Everything becomes so natural. Our bodies becoming one, all tangled in a mess of arms and legs, yet so beautiful. Our clothes glide off our bodies like butter. His mouth trickles around my body. Until he reaches between my thighs, I'm pretty sure the sheets are dripping from how bad I want this. His tongue spreading me apart.

Oh fuck.

Oh yes.

Oh Cole.

He is confident in the way he touches me, not surprised when I moan and smile. He knows what he's doing.

He comes up to my face, kissing me hard and fast, yet showing such tender and care in his touch. Caressing my body with all the attention it deserves. "You're so beautiful Ophelia." He moans between kisses. "Do you have a condom?" Cole asks as I rake my hands down his back, wanting more, wanting everything.

"Fuck. Yes. I think so." I briefly remember seeing a box of condoms in my bathroom drawer a month ago when I was unpacking everything. Cole rolls over onto his back, tucking his hands behind his head. I roll off the bed, running to the bathroom and rummaging through the drawers to find the box of condoms. Found them. They were in the back of the drawer next to an old eyeshadow palette that I keep meaning to throw away. We're kissing again, he pulls me onto his lap, my hips over his as he tears the condom wrapper open. His hands on my hips as he flips me back over, his teeth gently grazing my neck. His hands on me, stroking me gently. "Cole." I gasp, he looks up at me. "I want you inside of me now." I whisper.

Cole takes my hand from his shoulder. "Okay." He whispers back. Holding my hand in his.

We both gasp as he slowly slides inside me.

We look into each other's eyes before either of us move a muscle. "Are you okay?" He asks quietly.

I nod.

I forgot how fun and exciting sex was. I haven't had sex since May. I've missed it. Every noise we each make echoes in each other's ears making our own song up out of our moans and gasps. "Is this good?" He asks, his hand touching me right where I want it touch. My favourite part of sex is asking each other what's good and the check ins mid-way through, to make sure that we're both okay. I appreciate it. And I like that he's not doing it because he knows what I've been through, but he's doing it because he genuinely cares about how I'm feeling. My back arches as my hips press closer to his. His lips on mine, moaning into both our mouths, exchanging breaths. I am definitely living some women's dreams. Having sex with a man who reads romance, he knows exactly where to touch me, and when and knows when I'm about to finish, because that's when he lets himself relax and finish too.

Oh my god.

We're a mess of moans and fingernails in backs and hair and hands.

We lie next to each other on my bed, my ponytail splayed out around me, Cole catching his breath. "Oh my god, that was amazing." He exclaims. I want to turn over and hug him, but we're not that close yet. I know he has literally just been inside of me, but we're not emotionally close yet. Me and Blake were close before we had sex for the first time, maybe even too close, but it made after we had sex so much easier because we knew that we could hug right away and talk. It's just a little bit awkward right now. Like, I don't want Cole to leave right now, I want to hug him and talk to him, but we're not an official couple and is after care after sex reserved for relationships? "Are you okay?" He asks, turning over onto his side. I roll over so I'm facing him.

"I like cuddles after sex." I say, the petted lip out and the doe eyes staring at him. He shimmies closer to me, pulling the covers over us, he lets me lean my head on the inside of his arm while his other arm reaches around my body, casing me in, I tickle his back with my fingernails. "That was really good." I smile against his bare skin. His lips kiss my head. That was good. Really good. But I want to do it again. Cole's breath warm on my face, his fingers tickling my side. My favourite part of sex is afterwards. The cuddles, the pillow talk, the touching. The rerun of it in your head picking out your favourite bits.

"I know you're not looking for anything serious. But. I only have sex with people I'm serious about." Cole says. His fingers in my hair now.

"Me too." I whisper, yanking myself up to his lips.

I didn't want to go into anything serious. I didn't think I wanted anything serious. But I can't help but want that when I see Cole, when I think about him. We will take our time and get to know each other properly even though I feel like I've known him for years after just two dates and a coffee. But that's two dates and a coffee more than some.

Chapter 26

This is the first birthday I've had that I've spent alone. Well fully alone anyway. I don't have a bundle of presents sitting waiting for me. I don't have a cake. I don't have balloons. They always say that when you get older your birthdays become just like any other day. Well luckily its Sunday today. So, I can make it special. I sit in my house coat at the kitchen island with my cup of tea, debating whether or not to take myself out today for some lunch and a solo shopping date. *Like that's out of the ordinary for me.*

Knock knock

No one told me they were coming round; I would have put a bra on. Checking the peep hole. It's Dan.

"Happy birthday!" He exclaims, holding out a gift bag as he enters. Giving me an awkward side hug.

"Thank you." I cringe, retying the tie on my house coat to be sure that my boobs won't pop out.

"I'm only in for ten minutes, Lacy has me on a study schedule. She's got a wee something for you in there as well, she's stuck at university this week." I sit the bag on the kitchen bunker, I hate opening presents in front of people. Dan makes himself comfortable on the couch, laying fully back with his hands above his head on the arm of the couch. I sit on the pouffe, still with my tea in hand. "So, when am I meeting your mystery man then. I need to give him the stamp of approval." Dan likes to think that he is my father. But in reality, I'm his mother. I think me and Lacy have joint custody of him, always making sure that he's fed and watered, done his housework, done his homework. I'm sure that he's sick of us, but he does follow us around like a child most of the time, phoning at least one of us on a daily basis to act a basic question.

Knock knock

I sigh, its my birthday and I don't want to need to answer the door. "I'll get it." Dan huffs, swinging his legs around the side of the couch. "Hello?" I turn around hearing Dans confusion.

"Cole. Oh my god I didn't know you were coming." I smile rushing to the door. He looks upset, a sad '19' balloon and gift in his hands. His eyes scan between me and Dan. "Don't worry. This is Dan. I've told you about him."

His eyes brighten up. "Oh my gosh. Hi Dan, its so nice to meet you." He puts the balloons over to his other hand and shakes Dans hand.

"Nice to meet you, Cole. I'm just leaving the now anyway. See you soon. Don't break her heart, I'm a lawyer and I can cover up a murder. Bye Lia." He puts him on the back on his way out of the door.

"You'll not be a lawyer if you don't study." I lean over my front door shouting down the stairs. "Hi." As I turn my attention to Cole, my voice turns sweet and angelic. On my tip toes to give him a kiss, holding my house coat shut. Smiling up at the balloons. "Thank you." He holds me to him, smelling his fresh scent. I think its orange body wash that he uses. But sometimes it's lime. Either way. He is a very clean and fresh smelling man.

Closing the door behind us. "I genuinely thought I was going to need to punch someone there. And I've never punched anyone before, so I was panicking." He laughs. I take the gift and balloons from him and put them on the bunker next to the present from Dan and Lacy.

"Dan? Christ no, he was just dropping in to say happy birthday." I sit on one of my barstools, Blake comes and hovers over me, wrapping his arms around me tightly. The cold from outside clings to his hands.

"Happy birthday." He whispers.

"Thank you." Cole kisses my forehead; I close my eyes when he does. Tightening the tie of my house coat again. I should really invest in a new one that actually fits my boobs. "You didn't have to bring me a gift." I say as Cole slides a barstool next to me, leaning on the kitchen island.

"Yes, I did. It's your birthday and we're a couple… are we a couple. We haven't discussed our titles yet?"

This is the part of relationships that makes me cringe, the officiating of everything. "I would say that we're a couple. Is boyfriend and girlfriend an okay title for you?" Even though it sounds delinquently childish, there's no other words for two people who only sleep with each other and go out for dinner on a regular basis.

"That sounds great. Girlfriend." Cole leans in when he says girlfriend. Saying it as if we're six in the primary school playground. *Girlfriend.* I'm imagining people singing and tormenting us. *Cole and Ophelia sitting in a tree, K I S S I N G. there will not be a marriage nor a baby in a golden carriage.* For a long time. If ever. I don't think I ever want to get married. Is that something you should say to your, *boyfriend.* I'm not going to mention it.

that means planning a future. And my whole idea of moving was based on the fact that I didn't want to plan a future with someone else until I got to know myself a lot better.

"What are your big birthday plans for today?" Cole asks. Going into the fridge for a fresh bottle of water. That's another big thing about living in a city. Needing to buy bottled water. In small towns and villages, the tap water tastes delicious. And you could tell what street you lived on based on the water. Whereas in Glasgow the water tastes like metal dirt.

I hum and haw in my answer. It seems sad that my only birthday plans are to have a solo shopping trip and a lunch date. By myself. Like, I'm nineteen, other nineteen-year-olds are out with all of their friends in nightclubs and bars getting drinks bought for them. "Umm. I was just going to have a solo shopping and lunch date." I feel nervous and sad with my answer.

"Oh cute. Do you want me to go with you?" He asks, cracking open the bottle lid.

"No, it's okay. I was just hoping to spend some time with myself. Sorry, that sounds really rude. I just." I didn't mean for that to sound rude. Its just that when you spend so much time with other people you forget who you are, that's the reason I moved here, so I could have space and I feel bad saying no to people but I just need some alone time.

"Ophelia. it's okay. I was just asking if you wanted me to come. But if you want to have quality time with yourself that is perfectly okay." He takes my hand from the table and kisses it softly.

Because my birthday is in October, it, means that there's always an end of season sale at my birthday. It's a blessing and a curse, because it means that I will just go shopping. One of the things that I like doing when I go shopping by myself is try on bras in fancy bra shops, I've always loved doing that. One time, about a year ago I went in to get a new bra, but I wasn't sure of my size because I has lost a bit of weight and my boobs shrunk (thank God I felt like I was being devoured) and I went in and got a fitting, this woman was the sweetest woman to has ever walked the earth. And her name was Angel! How ironic. I always felt self-conscious going into those kinds of shops as a bigger girl but once I went in for the first time, I realised that everyone just wants to make you feel good. And the staff are so helpful, asking you if you need help finding a size, always complimenting your outfit, so chatty and bubbly. And it's what I look forward to every time I go shopping by myself.

I browse the racks of overpriced bras and body suits, of course I have a good rake through the sale bins of knickers. Seven for £30 that will do me just fine. I like to imagine myself being a sugar baby when I'm shopping, not worrying about the price because my rich sugar daddy will be paying for it all. Which may not be entirely false, I check my online banking account and Cole has sent me over £100 with the reference 'buy yourself something pretty for me to rip off of you' this man. This man. He knows what he's doing.

Me- Thank you baby xxx

Cole- You're welcome my queen xxx

Look at me giddily giggling in a bra shop. I do as he says.
I head into the fitting rooms to try on some things for him
to rip off me. This pink frilly number is calling my name,
its almost like a dress, I think it called a teddy? I've heard
that somewhere. The pink striped wallpaper in the fitting
rooms make the perfect background. Snapping a picture,
posing all pretty and all, making sure my boobs look
stunning, pushing them up to create the illusion of
silicone. Not that Cole cares.

**Cole- I can't deal with this, tell me when you're home
xxx**

I can imagine him right now, rolling his head back looking
at the picture, biting his lip. I can also imagine myself,
bent over the bed, the kitchen bunker, the couch. Okay get
to the tills now.

The happy cheery 'Valerie' scans my items through tills.
And she wishes me happy birthday. How cute. I take the
ribbon handles of the bag and skip out the shop.

As much as I want to sprint home and tell Cole that I'm
home and then pretty myself all up. I'm starving. Sitting at
a table for one in a restaurant used to be something that I
thought no one done and it was an awkward thing to do,
but since moving a couple of months ago, it's something
that I've grown accustomed to. There are so many
beautiful, delicious restaurants in Glasgow, and I would be
an idiot to not go into them just because I'm alone. My
comfort food is peri peri chicken. I always know what I'm
getting, medium butterfly chicken, spicy rice and
sometimes peri chips. I cut up the chicken and mix it in
with my rice and drench it in more medium sauce. The

one thing I don't like about his restaurant is that you can order free refill fizzy juice but need to sell a kidney to order a glass of water.

In my apartment I leap around dancing to my hype up playlist.

Me- I'm home xxx

Cole- I'll be 15 mins xxx

I always know when Coles excited because he forgets how to use words. If his boss saw him write 'mins' he would get sacked.

I sort my hair out, it's frizzy from my speed walk up here and tangled from sweat from trying on bras. And slip on my new cute, sexy, frilly night gown attire. How do you act sexy? Like when you know someone is coming over specifically for sex? Should I lie on the couch rose from titanic style? Should I just be in bed? I pour myself a glass of cheap wine and sit another glass out for Cole and hop onto the kitchen island. I can see a vague outline of Cole walking up the street from the window, but he can't see me. Flipping my hair and sipping on my wine.

Knock knock

"It's open!" I shout. Cole strolls it, closing and locking the door on the chain behind him before he looks at me. I pris my myself and cross my legs to look sophisticated.

"Fuck." He sighs biting and both licking his lips at the same time. Looking me up and down as he steps closer to me. I start to jump down off the counter. He grabs me mid air and tosses me back on to the counter. I laugh. He's smiling, tucking my hair behind my ear. Kissing me hard yet soft, his hands trailing my thighs. And he does what he said. Rips it off me. Well carefully removes it from me, it did cost him fifty quid. But I'll let him believe he ripped it off me.

Chapter 27

My fondness of Cole has grown every day I have known him, and I have known him a month. It was a month ago today that we met in the coffee shop. I trot my way down to the same coffee shop to surprise him. Ordering a bundle of cakes, a cinnamon latte and a hazelnut latte. The place still has the chilled-out buzz about it. I glance around when I'm waiting for the coffees, seeing couples sitting together, wondering if they're on their first date, wondering if in a months' time, a years' time, ten years' time, they'll be back in this coffee shop ordering the same things. Cole's apartment is quite literally right across from this coffee shop, his apartment used to be an office, I'm sure. There's him, his flat mate James and his other flatmate who I haven't met you who lives there. Its James' flat and he rents the rooms out. Buzzing the buzzer to get let in. "It's Ophelia." I shout, the doors get buzzed open for me. Staggering up the stairs, trying my best not to spill the coffees. Cole waits at his door for me. "Surprise." I say, out of breath from the stairs.

"Happy one month." He says, linking his arms under my arms and kissing my cheek. Taking the coffees from my hands whilst I get inside. Putting my jacket on the hooks by the door. It's a debate whether or not today is our official one-month anniversary because as much as we met that day and had coffee, we didn't have an official date until the Saturday, but we both agreed today that the day we met in the coffee shop is the official date. I slump myself on the couch whilst Cole fetches a plate for us to split the cakes in half like we did a month ago. James emerges from the hallway, probably smelling the sweet cakes.

"Morning." He scratches his face. It's 12pm. You would think that James is a teenager by the way he carries on, I've only met him a handful of times, anytime I'm over he always asks me for advice on women. But he's thirty. I thought that by thirty you would have your life sorted. I did think that about turning twenty though, and definitely not got my life together yet. I don't think it's a case of having your life together though. I think it's a case of being satisfied with your life and what you're doing with it.

Cole throws himself on the couch next to me as we dive into the cakes and pastries. He takes the remote and selects a movie. Coles favourite movie genre is world ending ones, natural disasters, that kind of thing. And he has got be hooked on them. My now insane ego believes that I would survive it. Huge tsunami? Just swim. Hurricane? Just hide underground. Killer monkeys? Make friends with them. James pinches one of the cakes and scurries to his room. Which gives us the opportunity to kiss. Loudly. Squealing as Cole pulls me on top of him. "Shut up." A muffled voice shouts.

"That's the other flat mate, he works nights." Cole sighs.

"I need to go anyways. I just wanted to see you." I kiss him one last time before I demount him and get my shoes back on. Cole kissing my shoulder as I do so. Turning back to face him. And kissing him again.

Chapter 28

Dear diary,

I love Cole. How terrifying is that. But I'm not scared. It's just a terrifying thing to admit. We've only been seeing each other for two months. But we're at each other's apartments every night, staying over at mine, mostly because I live myself and we can be as loud as we want. We have christened almost every room. I have only met one of Coles flat mates, he has two, but one of them works nights so I've never seen him. I don't actually know his name either. Cole is actually coming over tonight once he finishes work. But I love Cole. That was my point in this entry. Does he love me?

Love Lia

Xox

I stack up the pile of order forms on my standing desk. Whilst I wait for my cup of tea to cool down. Holding it in one hand, blowing it and glancing out the window, its super foggy outside today, so I can't see the ground, it's like I'm in literal heaven, floating on a cloud. I didn't go on my coffee walk this morning because it just looked so dreadful outside. The November cold has shocked me, the cold, chilly weather is my favourite, courieing yourself up with hats, scarves and gloves is so wholesome and comforting.

All orders are packed and ready to take to the post office, all piled up in a tote bag by the door. The post office staff hate me. I'll need to be sure to bring them a box of chocolates at Christmas. I wrap my scarf around my neck and pull my hat over my freshly washed hair. I just washed it last night, but I haven't straightened it yet, I'll be sure to do it tonight before Cole comes over in a few hours. I've never been someone who glams themselves up when they're around people, but I do like to feel my best most of the time, and to do that I like to have my hair neat and styled. I hate the stereotype of women sleeping in their makeup, waking up earlier to fix themselves up. If you really like someone and trust them and they really like you, they don't care what you look like.

"Hello my dear." Coles arms around my body, kissing my cheek. Closing the door behind him and locking it on the chain. He dumps the bag of snacks on the kitchen island, unpacking the bag. Cole enjoys bringing gifts, he never comes over without bringing me something, he's either seen a snack that he knows that I like, or a new book has been published at his work that he wants me to read. I have a stack of books on my shelves that he's brought me (definitely stole them from his work to be fair) and they're not even out yet and he has snuck them out.

"How was work?" I ask, getting him a drink from the fridge.

"New book that just came out today." He slides it across the island to me. A new cheesy romance. I inspect the cover. I'll add it to the collection that never stops growing.

"Thank you." Smiling flipping though the pages to smell the smell of new books. The smell reminds me of primary school. When you and you friend would go over to the bin and pretend to sharpen your pencils just so you could chat. That's what new books smell like to me.

The takeaway is ordered. We've been making our way through the entirety of Glasgow takeaways, every few days we'll order something. We decided to create a note in my note's app with the ratings of each one, time it took to get delivered, what we ordered etc, so we can give recommendations to people. All I want to tell Cole right now is that I love him. If you feel love for someone you need to tell them. But I don't think it can be a in a passing conversation, it should be a meaningful thing that you say meaningfully during a meaningful moment. I lie between Cole's legs, resting the back of my head on his stomach, feeling his body rise with every breath. He plays with my hair while I start reading one of the many books that he has given me. "I have waited for this all day." Cole sighs. Folding the page of the book and twisting myself around to face Cole. He grabs my chin gently and leans down to me kissing me softly, his hands grip around my waist and lift me up onto his lap. "Let me correct myself. I've waited for this all day." He smiles as I tickle the back of his neck. His lips part slightly, letting me slide my tongue in his mouth. The warmth of his lips is warming mine. Breathing each other in. His hands on my waist, reaching up my back under my hoodie. My hands on his shirt, trying to unbutton it one handed before he helps me. I reach my hands up as Cole pulls my hoodie over my head, throwing it onto the rug. Smiling as I tug at his sleeves to get his shirt off him. He begins to stand up, holding my hips tight as he picks me up. "Let's go to bed." He says. His hands on my booty as I kiss his neck.

"Yes please." I laugh. Gripping my body to him. He flops himself onto the bed, reaching up to throw the display pillows on the floor. All of my weight on him, arching my back as I kiss him. Running my hands up and down his abdomen, his hands at either side of me now. Fumbling around with his belt, struggling to unbuckle it. When I finally do manage to crystal maze style undo the belt Cole flips me over onto my back. I let out a laugh as he does so. He pulls my leggings off me, kissing the entire length of my leg, pulling me down to him at the thighs. His trousers are chucked across the room now, his belt almost smashing a vase in the process. Just our underwear between us now. I yank at my black knickers, using my feet to drag them down my legs. Edging Coles boxers down whilst I do so. Sitting up as Cole magics my bra clasps, kissing the surface of my boobs as he caresses my thighs. I love how he touches me. I love how he slowly pushes himself inside me. Waiting for me to grasp his back with pleasure. I love how he does that. He watches me adjust myself. I love how he does that. Groaning when he has pushed himself all the way in. I love how he does that. Holding a hand to my face as I moan. I love how he does that. I love Cole. "Wait wait wait." I stutter out as Cole's head drops to my shoulder.

"Are you okay? Do you want me to stop?" Cole immediately pulls out of me and backs away.

"No." I can feel the tears well up in my eyes. "I just." *Just say it, Lia.* I hold his head in my hands. "I love you." I pull my hands to my face, wiping the tears from my eyes.

I don't even want an answer, because no matter what Coles answer is, I love him. That feels so incredibly surreal to say out loud. Cole's silence is deafening. He pulls himself into my bare chest, then brings his face to mine.

"I love you too." His eyes glisten, tensing his cheeks to stop him from smiling too much. "I didn't want to be the first one to say it because I know you wanted to stay casual. But I love you." Inspecting each other's eyes, seeing our future in them. Our lips are together again. This isn't sex, this isn't making love, this is love. Like the dictionary definition of love, under the word you'll find this, just a picture of us on my bed, Cole holding my face to his, not wanting to miss a single millisecond of each other's presence, my legs wrapped around his hips, pulling him closer inside me. In a movie this is the part where the actors stop talking and music plays over them and the background is blurred.

My head resting on Cole's chest, his fingers running through my hair and his other hand holding mine. A blanket covering our waists, everything is silent apart from our breathing and the birds squawking outside. "Cole." I turn my head up to his, he twists his head down to me. "I can't promise that I'll love you forever, but I can promise to love you for as long as I can."

"I promise to love you for as long as you want me to." His lips meet my forehead.

I can't promise the future. I can't promise forever. All I can do is promise now.

Chapter 29

The takeaway didn't end up arriving last night, not that we would have heard the door going. Zero stars.

No one talks about how once you say 'I love you' to someone for the first time everything they do makes you want to say it. Snoring, I love you, farting in the middle of the night, I love you, when they get up in the morning to leave, I love you. I don't want Cole to leave my apartment. I want him to stay here and let me love him. I'm lying-in bed, still naked from the night before, with the duvet covering my chest, my hair looking like I've been dragged through a bush in the rain. Cole bends down to collect his clothes that the floor swallowed last night. "Cole. How about you just leave your clothes here?" I ask, rubbing the sleep from my eyes.

"Do you want me to have a drawer on something to have spare clothes in?" Cole buttons his wrinkled shirt.

"No. Do you want to live here?" That is something that I never in a million years would ask someone that. The reason I moved out alone was to become more independent and spend time by myself. I don't think about the words before I say them.

Cole pauses for a moment, contemplating his answer. "Yeah. I want to live with you." Saying it casually. Like it's a completely normal thing to say to someone. Inside I'm screaming with happiness. "I'll go pack my stuff." Sliding his shoes on.

"I'll come too." Leaping out of bed, trying to contain my excitement. We need a camera in here now. This is a new sit-com, comedy, romance, shit show.

Cole's apartment is massive compared to mine. There's three bedrooms and three bathrooms, everything is open concept, it's open concept to the point that it feels like a warehouse. I wave at James when I walk in, he's sitting in the living room munching on a bowl of cereal. If I'm staying here overnight, I struggle to sleep so I end up sitting in the living room, James will come in and he'll ask me for relationship advice. (James is a bit of a Casanova) "Hey James. I'm moving out." Cole says. James spoon smashes into the side of the bowl. "My rent is paid until the end of the month, so do you what you want."

"Oh okay." James goes back to eating his cereal.

I follow Cole through to his bedroom, he has an entire wall of books, like every single book he has ever read is on that shelf. He grabs a few bags and starts packing clothes in them. "Are you having a flitting?" I hear a way too familiar voice. I turn around. Almost in tears when I hear him. Him being Brian. He sees me, I don't think he recognises me. I recognise him though.

"Oh yeah, Ophelia, this is Brian." Cole motions between us. Brian holds out his hand for me to shake. I don't shake it. I don't look at it. I know how dirty those hands are. I am standing next to the man that ruined me. He broke me. My breathing becomes harsh when I go back to that night. With him. I can feel his hand holding out for mine. Then he walks away into the corridor. "Are you okay?" Cole asks, coming closer to me. "Look, if you're not ready for us to move in together that's okay." Cole rubs my arms for comfort.

"No, it's not that." That night is flooding back to me, the smell of whiskey on his breath, him towering over me, the kiss that was too cocky to be considered confident, the bruises around my wrists that I can still feel. "Are you friends with Brian?" Asking, my breath trembling.

Cole squints his face. "No not really, I just live in the room next to his." I have been having sex in a room next to Brian. He has probably heard us. He must have heard my name somewhere and thought 'oh shit I raped her', there's not too many Ophelia's in the world, unless I was one of many young women he ruined, and he didn't care to remember my name.

"Okay. I need to take care of something. Stay here." Taking a deep breath before I head out into the forest of a corridor, in search for Brian's presence. I see him, standing in the kitchen, watching the football game from afar. For years, I have done nothing but not want to see him again, be near him again, and here I am standing directly across from him in his apartment that he shares with my boyfriend. "Do you remember me?" I ask, he's still taller than me, still more built than me, but it's clear that he doesn't play rugby anymore because his muscles aren't so profound. He looks down at me confused. "You ruined me. You raped me. At my best friend's party. You broke me down to nothing. It's been two years and I can finally not feel your hands on me. You need to remember me."

He stares at me blankly, then looks over at James to notice if he has lifted his head from his cereal yet. He hasn't. "Oh

Ophelia, yeah, I remember you. That didn't happen though." I can see him start to sweat.

My anger erupts inside of me, but I keep it cool on the outside. "Brian. You raped me. You pinned me down by, my wrists and ripped my knickers off me, and you raped me, you came inside of me and left me there." My voice angry and stern, holding back the fear and tears that are slowly consuming me inside. "After I told you no. You left me in a bedroom at a party, you left right after, because you knew that what you done was wrong and you still did it. My best friend found me in a place that I don't want to be in again. I was at rock bottom. And I have worked so hard to be able to go back to a normal life and make something of myself…Been able to have sex without thinking of what you had done to me. You are not going to ruin me again. You are not going to ruin anyone else. But feel free to ruin yourself." Spinning around to get away from him, the adrenaline rushing to my brain. I see Cole hovering over the entrance to the living room staring at me. I walk straight past him and go out of the door without looking back. Because I know if I look back, I'll be seventeen again, and I'll be in Dans bedroom scared and hurting.

Cole chases after me on the main street, with four massive IKEA bags over his shoulders. "What was that? What happened?" I don't want to say it. I don't want that every time Cole looks at me to think that I'm just the one who was raped by his flatmate.

"Cole. If you love me, you'll not expect an answer." I stop storming away and stop, facing him. The tears are falling out of my eyes, and I don't realise. The adrenaline is still going.

"Okay." He whispers, taking a bag from one arm and putting it in the other, and wrapping that arm around me. "I love you."

"I love you too."

Clambering into Coles car with his stuff. I don't help him put the bags in the boot, which is something I would usually do, but he doesn't mind. When he gets in the car, he buckles his seatbelt, his hand on my knee. "It's okay…whatever it is, I still love you." I hate it when people say that. Because if I killed their family, they wouldn't still love me. He buckles his seatbelt and helps me buckle mine. Kissing my cheek once he clicks it in, because right now I can't do anything, but think. Think about Brian.

The drive from my apartment to Coles is five minutes, but it feels like a lifetime. I just keep replaying that night in my head. I feel like I'm seventeen again, questioning if I could have done something to stop him, what I did to provoke him? I need to shake myself. I am not the problem. Everything that Brian done to me has nothing to do with me and everything to do with him. "I need you to promise me something Cole."

"Anything."

"Promise me never to speak to Brian again." I still hate saying his name. "Don't ask why I just need you to promise me." I hold my pinkie up to Cole.

He wraps his pinkie around mine. "I promise."

I don't like keeping secrets from people. I don't want Cole to know how I know Brian. And it's not because I don't want to tell him because I do. I just don't want to end up being someone that he walks around eggshells with. I don't want to be someone that's whole personality is her trauma. I am so much more than what happened to me. I am successful. I am smart. I am kind. I am not the girl who was raped by Brian. I am Ophelia Opal Bloom. Independent, business woman who doesn't depend on anyone for her happiness. I believe it when I hear that Cole promises to not speak to Brian anymore. Because it would really hurt me if Cole lied and spoke to him again. And Cole doesn't want to hurt me.

Chapter 30

Christmas is in fourteen days. I'm determined to enjoy Christmas this year. I live with someone I love; I have an amazing job, I have hobbies that I partake in, I love my life now. My mum still hasn't met Cole. And she's far too busy in the salon in the lead up to Christmas to make time. She's not putting work before me or anything, she genuinely does not have the time to visit me so close to Christmas because she's working until nine most nights. She will have the chance to meet him on Christmas, I'm hosting a proper Christmas dinner this year. Dinner table and everything. It's going to be me, Cole, my mum, Dan and Lacy. I have finished my Christmas shopping and wrapping. The tree has been up for a couple of weeks because I got too excited. My life right now is amazing, my business is doing fabulous, Dan and Lacy are over around once a week for drinks, me and Cole go on weekly date nights, and I haven't had to think twice about myself. Our last date night a few days ago we went to the Christmas markets in town and spent a fortune on crepes and churros and nuts, we danced around to Christmas music and really got in the spirit of things. So, when I came home, I got the roll of pink and purple polka dotted wrapping paper out and became one of Santa's elves tying triple bows and all sorts of nonsense. It all looks an absolute mess but who cares, not me.

The apartment just looks so wholesome and festive. *It looks like two four-year-olds have decorated it right enough.* But wholesome and festive none the less.

"Bye my love." Cole rushes to me, throwing on his trench coat and sorting his collar out before he heads to work. kissing me on the cheek and running out the door.

"Bye my love." I shout back. Cole always runs late for work; he hasn't quite gotten used to the extra five-minute commute. It makes me feel a bit like a housewife, working from home, and because what I do is more of a hobby in terms of the fact that I enjoy doing it and it doesn't seem like a job when I'm doing it. I get to take my time in the morning, drinking tea, lounging around in my pyjamas before I start sorting out stock and orders. Things have been insane the past few weeks what with Christmas coming up. I released a Christmas collection of beanies and hoodies and sold out within two days! That was many sleepless nights of work packing orders and running back and forth to the post office. I released stickers and notebooks too, which have quickly become my favourite things to package, because its so easy to do. I wanted to design a collection for Christmas that reminds everyone that Christmas and Hanukkah and all other holidays that its okay to gain weight. None of that 'loosing the Christmas weight' bullshit around here.

Cole usually finishes work at four most nights, so I normally take my orders down to the post office and meet him on the way, sometimes we pick up dinner or a takeaway hot chocolate since they have the Christmas flavours out now. My favourite one I've tried is the chocolate orange one.

I'm comfortable in my life now. There's never a moment where I wonder what's happening or wonder if I'm alone again. Because I'm not. Me and Cole are basically joined at the hip. And we're not getting sick of each other yet. I don't think I'll ever get sick of Cole. We were made from the same mould. Cut from the same piece of fabric. Whatever one of those sayings. Life is great with Cole.

I pick Cole up from work and wander around the Christmas markets for what feels like hundredth time this month, glugging down lethal Buckfast mulled wine. His arm around me, my bobble hat tickling his chin. Looking at all of the ice skaters, some falling and some doing tricks. I think that's the best way to describe life. Watch people ice skate.

Chapter 31

Waking up on Christmas morning and I feel like a child again. Cole rolls over to me and hugs me tightly, his head on my shoulder and his bare arms trailing around my stomach. "Merry Christmas." He says in his sleepy voice.

"Merry Christmas." I twist around, taking his head in my hands. Kissing his lips, embracing the morning breath. We lie for a minute, taking in the moment. I feel whole. Like I have finally found the missing piece of my puzzle. I pass Cole his glasses from the bedside table. He squints as he struggles to put them on, rubbing his face with his thumbs. "Can we open presents now?" I say like a child, flashing the doe eyes.

"Yes, let's go." Cole races out of the bed, throwing the covers back at me when I try to race him. I laugh flinging myself back into bed and going around the side of the bed like an adult. *It's not fun being an adult.* In the living room Cole has picked out his first present to open, sitting on the rug next to the tree cross legged with the present on his knees. I know exactly what it is. It's a new pair of trainers that he asked for, they sold out months ago and I hunted high and low for them but finally found them on a sketchy website. They're probably fake but it's the thought that counts. "I need my cup of tea before I do anything." I laugh, tying my house coat shut, going into a cupboard to get a mug.

"You're no fun." He says sarcastically crossing his arms in a huff.

I think about it for a second. Why am I acting like this? It's fucking Christmas, all rules of life are struck off. When you get the opportunity to act like a kid again, do it. I slam the mug on the worktop and rush over to the tree, picking out a present to open. Shaking it to try and hear what it is. We both laugh until we're a bundle of kids on the floor. We both told each other that we were setting a three-gift limit which Cole has not followed in the slightest. I have, but that's because his shoes were so expensive. Cole bought me a beautiful necklace; its silver and it has a cloud on it. its such a me piece of jewellery. I hate love heart shaped jewellery. I made that very clear to him. And a bundle of facemasks, body creams and washes, of course new pyjamas and candles, it's me you're talking about here. The other gifts I got Cole are a new pair of pyjamas and a body wash set. The classic gifts. We spend a good hour on the floor admiring the gifts, just like when you're young, you sit on the floor and play with your new toys until dinner time. We put a Christmas movie on the projector in the background to have some noise going.

Something I never done on Christmas was get glammed up. Christmas was always a time where we would stay in comfy clothes all day and not care what you look like. I never realised that other people got fully dressed on Christmas until a few years ago. So, the red lipstick is on, red dress and bows in my hair. My makeup is looking flawless as ever with my new blush on that I *might* have bought for myself when I said I was Christmas shopping.

The Christmas crackers are on the table, I bought extra fancy ones with not only jokes and paper hats but mini sewing kits and mini screwdrivers. The Christmas tree is pristine, well as pristine as a bright pink tree can be, the tree itself is green and frosted but all of the ornaments are bright pink and tacky. Just the way I like it. It's my first Christmas tree so it was very important to me that I could let my inner child loose. My tree at my mums was always pink, but classy pink with crystal decorations and absolutely zero tinsel because my mum thought it was disgusting and tacky. I've pinned stands of tinsel around my windows that still don't have blinds or curtains. I've grown to like the fact that I can look out and see everything so I'm not going to get curtains or blinds. And Cole doesn't seem to mind it. He's cutting up all the potatoes and parsnips. A god-awful number of parsnips. I hate them, but my mum loves them so I promised her we would serve them. The bin bag of ripped wrapping paper sitting at the door and the snow falling like dusted sugar onto the ground outside. I fling the chicken in the oven, because it should be illegal to serve turkey. You don't eat it throughout the year because no one likes it, so why do we dedicate a full day of the year to eating it?

Mum- I'll be 30 mins. Xx

Me- Okay xx

"Okay my mum is on her way. This is the first time she's meeting you so you need to make sure that she likes you right off the bat, she is very good with first impressions, and she will hold it against you for the rest of your life." I point my finger at Cole while he oils up the pans. "I'm sorry, I'm rambling, and stressing and I need to sit down." I pull up a barstool at the kitchen island and hold my head in my hands.

"Okay Ophelia. Relax. Your mum is not going to hate me. It's Christmas." He clearly has no idea. "Look. Dan and Lacy will be here soon too, and they adore your mum, and they also adore me." He says cockily. I shake my head. Going onto the couch, fluffing up my pillows and making sure that the Christmas tree looks perfect even though it's coming down tomorrow. I can't stand it when tree is up too long after Christmas. Christmas stresses me out enough what with the mess that it leaves afterwards. I can already feel the bin bag at the door taunting me. Watching me to make sure that it's not going to sit for any longer.

Knock knock

I rush over to the door, welcoming Dan and Lacy with my arms.

"I'm freaking out over here Lacy." I whisper into her ear as I hug her.

"Merry Christmas to you too." She says sarcastically. Mocking my frustrations.

We exchange gifts and boxes of chocolates. Scattering dishes of chocolates around the living room and kitchen to have throughout the next fortnight. That's the thing with getting gifted boxes of chocolates, every time you pass them you take a handful. We get some much-needed pictures by the tree, posing with our very snazzy Christmas outfits on. Outside is so picturesque. The streets are empty, but I can peek into the flats and see everyone, all doing the same thing as us, preparing for dinner and gathering around the tree to take pictures.

Knock knock

It's my mum, I run over to the door, looking back to make sure the apartment looks perfect, ushering Cole over to me so we can both greet her at the door. He prances over next to me, running the palms of his hands over his red jumper to even out any creases. I take a deep breath before I open the door.

I smile when I see her, throwing my arms around her. "Hi mum." I say with tears in my eye for some reason. "Merry Christmas" hugging her tight.

"Merry Christmas Ophelia." She kisses my cheek; her hair has a light layer of snow on top of it from her short walk from her car. I let my mum breathe again when I let her go.

I wave my hands over to Cole. "Hello Cherry, I'm Cole, its so nice to finally meet you." He says just like we rehearsed it over and over again last night.

Mum throws her arms around Cole, catching him off guard. "It's so nice to meet you, Cole." She kisses his cheek too. This is so not the reaction I expected from my mum, I don't know why. I assumed that she would freak out about it. Because things have moved super speedy between me, and Cole and she hadn't had a chance to meet him. maybe she got Dan to be a spy and check him out for her. Which definitely sounds like something my mum would do, and Dan would absolutely agree to any of my mums' master plans.

Me and Cole stare at each other in shock when she hugs Dan and Lacy. "That went well." Cole puts his thumbs up before I shut the door. Mum treats Dan and Lacy like her other children. Even when we were young, always made sure that they were okay, if we were going out anywhere, asked if they wanted to go. Like congratulations Ophelia, you're the third favourite child. She puts a bundle of presents under the tree. Getting her snowy coat off her and putting it on the coat stand at the door.

"Everything looks amazing Lia. I'm so proud of you." She speaks. I'm still standing at the door, not quite knowing how to act in this situation. This is another part of romantic comedy movies that I skip because it's too cringey.

"Thank you." I reply. I shake myself and get back into the kitchen with Cole while everyone makes their selves comfortable.

I display all the food on the island like a buffet so people can just get what they want. Patch passing plates and cutlery around, and I don't want to sit beside a bowl of parsnips.

"Okay everyone. Help yourselves." I shout as I sit the plates on the side of the island. This is the part of Christmas in movies that seemed stressful and overwhelming to me. Being around everyone and eating dinner. Scooping potatoes and pulling apart the chicken while Cole finishes setting the table.

We set the table up like an actual proper dinner table. I didn't think I wanted a dinner table until I realised, I needed one when I decided to host dinner. I've got me on one side of the table and Cole at the other, then my mum and Lacy next to each other and Dan opposite them. I feel weird sitting at a dinner table eating. I've never done it unless I'm in a restaurant. I always just eat on the kitchen island staring at the cupboards or on the couch watching friends. I mirror Coles movements by placing the napkin on my knees. "Are you okay." Cole mouths as everyone begins to sit down.

I nod. Am I? Who knows at this point?

"Well done guys this all looks amazing." Dan says squeezing in his chair, with half a Yorkshire pudding already in his mouth. I see Lacy shake her head out of the corner of my eyes. I smile leaning my head down.

"Right, tuck in." I announce.

What are good dinner conversation topics? What do people speak about whilst having dinner? Do you speak during dinner?

"Did Ophelia tell you about how we first met, Cherry?" Cole asks. I smile again. "It was at one of the coffee shops down in the town centre. I went up and ordered us more coffee and got us some cakes too. And I brought a cherry Bakewell. But Ophelia is allergic to cherries. When I found out your name was Cherry I died laughing." He laughs now thinking about it.

"Oh my god I know. I've got a four-year-old swelling up in accident and emergency screaming 'she cant be allergic to cherries, that's her mother's name!" Her and Cole continue the conversation, Lacy and Dan join in too, but I stay silent not because I don't want to join it, because I do. But I'd rather just watch it happen and fully appreciate the moments. Some people don't get many moments like this. I grew up with a family that as much as they loved me, I didn't feel as if they did. I grew up with two parents who loved each other until they had me. I always thought that I was the problem, and I was the catalyst in their separation. I don't remember having a Christmas like this one. It was always just me and my mum, around the kitchen island eating a cook in the bag roast chicken with frozen roast potatoes and parsnips that made me feel sick looking at them. After dinner we would go our separate ways and do as we please. We never played board games or talked. Like actually talked. Christmas was always that time of year when I felt the most alone. My mum felt the same way. And it's not like we didn't want to spend time together, because we did. We just didn't know how to be together at Christmas. My mum hated Christmas growing up as well. Her family would sit around the dinner table and pretend to like each other while playing with dry turkey and overcooked peas that no one ate, the smell of cigarettes clinging to her clothes and filling up on ritz crackers and squirty cheese. She promised me that I would never have a Christmas where I would have to be around a family that didn't like each other. And as much as she tried, she couldn't help me have a family Christmas. Well now. I'm nineteen. And I have a family Christmas. It may not have aunties and uncles and blood relatives. But a nerdy big brother who would go to the end of the earth to help me, a scientist sister who is way to pretty and fashionable to be a scientist, a goofy, clever, boyfriend who just wants to love me, me a hot mess business woman who couldn't tell you the last time she has took her anti-depressants. And a mum who after thirty-seven years has finally had a proper family Christmas with a family that love each other. It may not be perfect for everyone. But it's perfect for me.

I would say that dinner was a success. Empty plates and empty trays, everyone went up for seconds. There were no arguments, there were engaging conversations, the Christmas cracker jokes got everyone smiling. Cole scrapes the burnt bits off the bottom of the trays and stacks them up at the sink. Dan and Lacy make their way to the couch and clink on my laptop to set it up to the projector. Its tradition for me to watch back to the future one and two at Christmas time. Not three though, it's not as good as the other ones. Even though back to the future isn't a Christmas movie I always watched it at Christmas growing up, they always played them on channel five. I put on my marigolds and make a start to the never-ending pile of dishes; Cole wipes down the table and island. "So?" I ask my mum when she trots over to the sink dumping some of the dishes on the worktop as I rinse the congealed gravy off them, turning to her slightly, not too obviously.

 She looks behind her making sure that Cole isn't near her. "He's great Ophelia. You're glowing differently. You're yourself around him. It's a good thing. And he really loves you" She whispers into my ear in a way that seems like she means it. "And you love him too, don't you?"

"I really do mum." I really do.

We spend the next few hours on the couch and the beanbag chairs drinking cocktails and playing 'who am I' you know that game where everyone has a celebrity's name on their head, and you need to guess which celebrity you have on your head. I have Adele on mines, I guessed it within three questions. One- am I a singer? Two- am I a woman? Three- am I Adele? I'm smiling too hard right now. Seeing the four closest people in my life be so happy with each other and smiling and laughing and just generally enjoying being around each other. It's the best Christmas present I could have ever asked for.

I escape to the bathroom for some much-needed deep breaths. Dabbing my under eyes with toilet roll not to ruin my mascara with teary eyes. Skimming through social media, sitting on the edge of the bath. I see him. I see Blake. Him and his girlfriend next to the Christmas tree in their flat. I'm happy for them. And I'm sure Blake thinks the same thing when he sees the pretty much identical picture me and Cole took earlier. They look really happy together. So do me and Cole. We both found someone we could fall hard for. I'd be lying if I said that I didn't hate myself one tiny bit for letting Blake go. He is such an amazing man. But I couldn't let myself fall. Not hard enough anyway. I don't think Blake is the kind of man I can fall for the way I have fallen for Cole. Cole is funny, goofy, makes me feel like a child again, and he loves me. So much. And I love him. So much. I'm glad I let myself fall for Cole. I think I might have tripped, stumbled and somersaulted in love with Cole.

Chapter 32

Everyone has left and the apartment now feels empty. Dan brought the rubbish down the stairs with him so I wouldn't have to look at it any longer. I have had my Christmas bubble bath with my new fancy bubble bath that my mum bought me. Cole meets me in the bedroom. Flaunting his new look. My mum got me and Cole matching Christmas pyjamas, they are the traditional 'Christmas pattern' zig zags and polka dots, red, white and green. He kicks each leg to the side strutting his stuff. He tosses the matching pair to me from the other side of the bed.

Slipping them on and braiding my hair. My childhood is coming back to me now. Anytime I wear my hair in pleats I feel young. The Christmas movies are still on a loop in the living room when I go out, showing off my pyjamas and shimmying and dancing along to the music in the movies, Cole spinning me around and dipping me to kiss me. Just like in the movies. The both of us smiling and laughing our heads off. Cole goes over to the dinner table and takes one of the Christmas cracker hats for each us. I cackle when he places it on his head, still boogieing. We both go around the apartment and throw away any sign of mess and wipe everything down. It's right now, while me and Cole are dancing in our Christmas pyjamas cleaning up for the second time tonight, singing to Christmas songs and watching Christmas movies in the background that I realise. True love really does exist. Love, it exists in every shape or form. Love is ordering a fancy coffee just because you want to, waking up early to make a special breakfast so your day starts a little better, love is the overwhelming sensation you feel when you can't use any other word to express how you feel. Wither that be for a coffee or for another person.

"Thank you." I look over at Cole, still with his Christmas cracker hat on.

"For what?" He replies. Reaching down the back of the couch to get the scraps of wrapping paper from under the cushions.

"For showing me that love exists" I can love someone, and it doesn't mean that I'll lose myself. I can love someone unconditionally. And not fear the future because the future hasn't happened yet, and the future isn't promised. So, I should love someone for as long as the future allows me to.

Cole smiles softly, we shuffle over to each other, dancing while we hug closely, looking out of the window at the beautiful snow that is dusting the city.

Dear diary

It was me. I was the one holding myself back the whole time. I was the one who was terrified that I wasn't enough for someone. It was me who was too scared to tell the people I love that I love them. But it was Cole who showed me that it's not scary to love. It was Cole who showed me that love doesn't need to end in tears. Love, It's beautiful. So yes Lia. Love really does exist. It always has.

Love Lia.

Xox

Epilogue

Dear diary,

Long time no see. I'm twenty-two now. If I'm being honest, I completely forgot about you. I apologise. I found you in the back of my desk when I was packing. I'm moving. We're moving. Me and Cole are moving into a three-bedroom house, you know the house that I never seen myself living in. That one.

In the three years since I've written in here so many things have happened. I've got a rock on my finger! Again, something that I never thought would happen. Cole proposed on our one-year anniversary in that coffee shop that we met in. it was definitely one of the cringier moments in my life.

Self-care co has slowly taken over the world. (Just a bit dramatic there) but I have a few little boutiques that sell vintage clothing that stock my stuff now which is insane. What is even more insane is that I wrote a book! It's a self-care, self-love, self-acceptance book. I had a hard time with life up until about now to be honest and I wanted to help people and make them feel good. So that's what I done. Cole definitely pulled some strings at his work to get me published.

I'm pregnant! I'm seven months along. With a little girl. The real reason I pulled you out of my bedside table right now is because I can't sleep. I can't sleep because I'm thinking. Cole is snoring his head off next to me, with one hand on the bump. And I can't stop thinking about how glad I am. I'm so glad I kept going.

Love Lia

Xox

Acknowledgements

Thank you.

Thank you to my amazing clients who have supported me throughout this process.

Thank you to my Gran Cooper. You always made me feel like I was worth something. 'you're really good with your words' is what you always told me. All those afternoons on your computer growing up and writing stories about horses came to something.

 Thank you to my great uncle Doe. You were more than a great uncle to me. You were my papa. You made me feel amazing. You were always there for me even when I wasn't there for myself.

Thank you, Laurie. For both being my very professional editor and correcting spelling mistakes for me which I'm not going to lie, made me feel like you were my teacher. And for also just being an amazing person and someone that I can always count on.

Mrs Bernstein. My third- and fourth-year art teacher. When I left school all those years ago you were sad because I wasn't going to study writing. Here you go Mrs B. Thank you for believing in me.

Most importantly thank you to everyone who said I couldn't do it. If I'm one thing. I'm determined, if you say

I can't do something. I'll do it ten times bigger and throw it in your face.

And you know what. Thank you to me. For actually sitting down and starting this and finishing it. Go me.

Thank you to everyone who has purchased, borrowed, stole this book. Share it with everyone. Friends, family, enemies. Because everyone deserves to know that they are loved.

Started 20th August 2022-finished 11th January 2023

Printed in Great Britain
by Amazon

16701451R00119